MAPS TO DEATH

The Ticonderoga Experience

MAPS TO DEATH

JOHN SIELA

iUniverse LLC
Bloomington

Maps To Death
The Ticonderoga Experience

iUniverse books may be ordered through booksellers or by contacting:

iUniverse LLC
1663 Liberty Drive
Bloomington, IN 47403
www.iuniverse.com
1-800-Authors (1-800-288-4677)

Because of the dynamic nature of the Internet, any web addresses or links contained in this book may have changed since publication and may no longer be valid. The views expressed in this work are solely those of the author and do not necessarily reflect the views of the publisher, and the publisher hereby disclaims any responsibility for them.

Any people depicted in stock imagery provided by Thinkstock are models, and such images are being used for illustrative purposes only.
Certain stock imagery © Thinkstock.

ISBN: 978-1-4759-6343-4 (sc)
ISBN: 978-1-4759-6344-1 (e)

Library of Congress Control Number: 2012922091

Printed in the United States of America

iUniverse rev. date:10/25/2013

Contact John Siela at
jsiela@onlyinternet.net

In loving memory of my two sons,
Rick and Randy, and my grandson, Landon.

Acknowledgments

I would like to express my deep appreciation to my wife, Jean, who has been so patient with me during the process of writing this book. Also to my two sons, Ron and Rudi, who have been encouraging me to continue my dream.

Thank you also to the professional, computer support of Sheri James, to Tom Fean for his direction, to Lesley Wright for her artistic work as a graphic designer, and to Pam Siela for her computer assistance.

I also thank my Lord and Savior, to Whom I owe everything.

A Note From The Author:

As I sat at my desk, recently retired, I wondered, "What now?" I picked up the familiar yellow pencil on my desk and rolled it between my fingers. I had contemplated writing a book before, but had dismissed it as an impossible dream. On this day, however, that dream seemed achievable. I had always loved mysteries, and an idea now swirled around in my head. First I needed a name for the main character and a setting for the story. I turned my pencil over in my hand and looked at the engraving that I had seen a hundred times before, "Dixon Ticonderoga" . . . and so was born the main character, Dixon. The name, Ticonderoga, made me think of a deep, dark forest in Canada. The name and setting were perfect for my novel . . . Maps to Death, The Ticonderoga Experience.

Thank you, Dixon Ticonderoga Company, for inspiring me. I have used your product throughout my life . . . as a child at school; as a young man writing love letters to my wife while serving in the military; as an adult in the workforce; and now, as a retiree, writing my first novel. The longevity of the Dixon Ticonderoga Company proves their product is a quality pencil, produced by a quality company.

-John Siela

Chapter 1

It was early winter. Snow was falling heavily on the Ticonderoga. Dixon, fearing the worst, continued to chop wood for his heating stove. Nightfall would soon consume the light of day, and for a moment, Dixon enjoyed the thought of settling down for the night. As that moment passed, he realized that he had not thought of food since breakfast. It would soon be too dark to consider hunting. His aching body was too tired to even consider venturing out on this night.

He finished stacking the wood he had cut and loaded his strong arms with enough logs to keep his cabin warm all night. The snow kept falling as he poked the red embers in his old heating stove. In his cabinets, he found some canned sauerkraut and some canned beef. He threw them together, and the aroma was surprisingly appetizing. He cleaned his mess, made some strong coffee, and sat down in his old wooden rocker with the bearskin for a cushion. This would be a good night to study maps, he pondered, as he lit up his pipe and drank his coffee.

Dixon was beginning his third winter on the Ticonderoga. He and his wife, Chris, had once lived in a modest Cape Cod in Dovel, Maryland, near Baltimore. Irish American like Dixon, Chris was an intelligent, attractive, and fun-loving wife. The two of them had a good marriage—they enjoyed each other's company and the building of their dreams. They enjoyed the same things and often would go camping and hiking. They were both very good marksmen and would hunt together, eating what they killed on their camping trips. They had often discussed visiting the Ticonderoga, where they could enjoy all their interests.

Chris' grandfather had been a licensed pilot and involved in international trade with foreign countries. He left Chris quite wealthy at his death. When he was killed, she also came into possession of some maps of Ticonderoga that he'd kept hidden in a lockbox. The young couple had not understood what the maps represented but realized they must be of some importance or her grandfather would not have locked them away. They had always been fascinated with the region, and when the maps surfaced, it thoroughly intrigued them.

Dixon O'Laverty was a well-respected architectural designer in Dovel and enjoyed his work immensely. But Chris was acutely aware they weren't getting any younger as they moved into their late thirties. She gently pushed her husband, urging him with remarks like "Dixon, when are you going to put your pencils down and take us on a long vacation?"

Dixon had finally gotten around to making those plans to visit the Ticonderoga for an extended camping excursion when he was jolted with the worst event of his life—and the tragic end of his beloved wife's. He arrived home from a business trip to police cars and paramedics and Chris being wheeled out on a gurney . . . with a sheet covering her body. She had been found mysteriously murdered in their home. He was never a suspect; his alibi and distress were unmistakable, but Dixon delayed no further. Even though her murder remained unsolved, Dixon decided to leave the house and the life they'd shared in Dovel and move straightaway to the Ticonderoga of their dreams.

Chapter 2

T he Ticonderoga, located in the northern Canadian territories, contained over four hundred thousand acres of pines, hardwoods, a river, bear, deer, and many other varieties of wildlife that roamed the woods. He missed Chris desperately, but Dixon's new life of hard work, scrabbling day to day just to keep food on the table and essentials available, helped him get through the grief of his loss and the rage toward her nameless murderer. By the start of the third year, he could even say his life had become exciting and enjoyable.

Despite the hard work, Dixon loved the life on the Ticonderoga. He learned the habits and instincts of the wildlife. He learned how to survive in the outdoors for days at a time in subfreezing temperatures. Although he depended on wildlife to sustain his own being, he respected the animals that owned these woods. He had never killed an animal just for sport, only for food. And finally he was comfortable and confident in being able to survive.

Now he was ready to take action on those maps that had fueled his and his late wife's fascination. He had studied them plenty but had been unable to locate their starting point or any similarity in the landscape he now knew to the directions that were defined on them. He was looking forward to the coming spring when, with his friend Cody, he would be exploring the Ticonderoga in a helicopter. As Dixon studied the maps, his mind reflected back to when he and Chris would pull them from their old safe and look at them for hours.

They knew they would not be able to understand the guidelines and directions without actually being on the Ticonderoga, but enjoyed just imagining what mysteries might lay ahead of them.

It had been just two years to the day since Chris had picked up the maps from the lockbox. Dixon was attending a meeting in Boston. Chris had a hair appointment in the morning, a luncheon date with her best friend and neighbor, and then a three PM dental appointment. When she was late for the dentist, the dental office called her home. There was no answer. Her friend and neighbor—their backyards shared a fence—Tara Copely, knowing that Chris might be recuperating from her dental work, made some hot soup to take to her house. When she arrived and Chris did not answer the door, Tara, thinking Chris had not returned from her appointment, used her keys to Chris' house to go in. Tara did not notice anything unusual in the house as she found a pan, poured in the soup, and turned the burners on low.

As Tara went into the family room to sit down and wait, she noticed the door leading to the lower level was open about six inches. Tara knew that Chris always kept that door shut. Maybe she's downstairs, Tara thought.

"Chris?" called out Tara as she opened the door just before she gasped at the sight. She could only see Chris' arms lying on the basement floor, but she knew it was bad. She screamed, "Chris!?" and immediately knew she must call 911. Tara did not go downstairs until the paramedics arrived. It was not until then that the realization of a bizarre murder had occurred.

The paramedics found Chris bludgeoned to death; but before she was killed, she had been tortured. Burns were evident all over her body, prompting the paramedics to call the police.

Unlike the main level, the basement had been ransacked. The police surmised that the intruder or intruders wanted access to the safe. It was a large antique safe, too big to move, and required knowledge of the combination to open. They also surmised that since the intruders could not find a written combination, they attempted to get it from Chris by torturing her, but without success. The safe remained closed and locked.

Neither Tara nor the police could conceive what would be so valuable in the safe that Chris would not open it for the intruders. At six PM, Dixon received a page from his office to call home. When Tara answered, Dixon realized something was wrong. With as strong a voice as Tara could muster, she told Dixon that he must return to his home immediately. "Okay," said Dixon, "but what's wrong, Tara? Is Chris all right?" asked Dixon, and Tara broke down. She handed the phone to Police Chief Ted Hands, with whom Dixon was acquainted. Ted informed Dixon of Chris' death. Dixon arrived home at four AM. Ted Hands was there to greet him.

Ted informed Dixon what the police department had perceived about what might have occurred prior to Chris' death. He asked Dixon what was in the safe and who knew about it.

Dixon, tired and in shock, told Ted that they only kept personal items in there, bank statements, credit card information, and such. He said there was very little money in the safe—a few hundred dollars of emergency cash. He could not imagine what anyone thought might be valuable enough to murder for it. The next few weeks, Dixon went through the normal grieving process, always wondering who and why this terrible thing could happen to his Chris.

Chapter 3

It was not until two months later, as Dixon was going through the items in the safe, that he came across the maps that he and Chris had so often looked at. As he was reviewing the maps, it suddenly occurred to him that these maps could be the reason why the intruders broke into the house. *Were the intruders somehow aware that these maps were in Chris' possession? Would the maps contain a value of some type that people would torture and kill Chris for?* Dixon couldn't imagine that such a value existed. Yet, he wondered, *If there was some type of monetary value, why wouldn't Chris' grandfather have shared this information with Chris, as they were very close?*

As the months passed, Dixon thought of her continually. He could not get her life or her death out of his mind. He decided it was time to take a leave from his employment and visit the Ticonderoga. He had to discover the mysteries of the maps.

Chapter 4

Dixon never shared with anyone the fact of his possession of the maps—not the police, not Tara, not anyone. Although he and Tara had remained close friends, Dixon told her only that he planned to take a year's leave to travel. Tara agreed to take care of Dixon's home, as nice rentals were scarce in this small college community. Dixon told Tara that he would contact her periodically and apprise her of his location.

With warm weather approaching and plans completed with Tara on the rental of the house Dixon headed for Ticonderoga, first by commercial air and then by small plane, a puddle jumper. After three stops on the puddle jumper, Dixon boarded a small motor boat and settled down for a long ride. When they arrived at the dock, the boat's owner said that he would stop by in three months and waved good-bye as he left Dixon on an isolated area in the Ticonderoga.

Bushwhacking his own path, it took Dixon two days to travel six miles. He estimated that he had reached the approximate center of the Ticonderoga forest. This is where he would build his cabin.

Dixon found out quickly that he wasn't as ready for this type of life as he thought he was. The nights were colder than he expected. He put together a small stove that he had brought with him, but he intended to have a small cabin built before winter. With the ordeal of clearing his site, cutting down enough trees of the right size to build—with a camp saw and an ax—dragging them to the site with ropes, and hunting for food, winter was fast approaching. He knew his days were limited. Energized by his thoughts of Chris and the reason he was here, he worked harder and longer to get his cabin nearly complete.

At one time, he contemplated going back with the boat when it returned in about four weeks. But as the scheduled arrival approached, Dixon could feel himself getting stronger, wiser, and more confident in himself. He had always been athletic and strong—he'd had to be. He was raised on a Virginia farm, and his father had died when he was nine years old. Dixon had learned to farm, hunt, shoot, and take care of himself and his mother at a young age. He decided to look at his current situation as something he'd trained for.

When the guide with the boat returned, Dixon was almost done with his cabin. He trekked the six miles to the dock and picked up his supplies, including food and plenty of ammunition for the winter. The guide gave Dixon a three-year Lake George calendar as an early Christmas gift and informed him that he would not be returning until next spring. He wished Dixon good luck as he headed back to civilization.

Dixon's first winter was not easy. He had stored fruits and berries in a pit that he had dug. The pit would keep the fruits and berries from freezing. One morning he discovered that bears had dug up the pit. They had eaten or destroyed all Dixon had stored. He had not dug the pit deep enough.

He kept track of the days on his calendar, imagining what his colleagues and clients would be wanting from him if he'd stayed in the suburbs. On New Year's Eve, it was extremely cold, much colder than usual. Dixon packed his stove early and knew he would need to repack it in the night. When he awoke with the frigid air to do so, one of the logs was too long for the door to completely close. Dixon was sleepy, cold, and in a hurry to get back into his sleeping roll. He didn't notice the door was not closed tight. Just before dawn, he was awakened to a fiery inferno. One end of the cabin was being consumed and beginning to spread.

He grabbed large blankets and began beating down the flames. He couldn't afford a disaster like this! Just then, part of the roof caved in, and the snow from the roof fell on the flames. Fate had dealt him a stroke of luck. The heavy snow and his efforts with the blankets put the fire out. He used the canvas from the tent that he had used while building his cabin to close up the gap the fire had made. The next morning, he covered the outside of the tent canvas with pine boughs. His sweat-and-tears-built cabin was now half tent again, but at least he would keep warm enough until spring.

Chapter 5

A gain it was hard work that kept him alive. Hunting and salting meat, chopping wood, and fireproofing kept him warm. The months went by. As warm weather was approaching, Dixon attempted to set his priorities. He now realized that living on the Ticonderoga required most of his time just for the essentials. He originally planned to read, hike, and study the maps. He found he had little time for any of those.

He would rebuild the cabin and dig a deeper and more secure pit for his fruits and berries. He would purchase all the food supplies his boat guide could spare. The less food he had to hunt for the more time he would have to explore and study. Dixon knew the coming year would be better and, he hoped, easier. He couldn't wait for warmer weather.

Spring arrived late on the Ticonderoga. Dixon started repairing his cabin before warm weather arrived. He was anxious to complete the project before the guide arrived, which should be soon, when Dixon would have to hike the six miles from his cabin to the meeting place. When he figured the guide would be arriving anytime within the next two weeks, he took his fishing gear, rifle, and what was left of his tent, and headed to the lake.

Chapter 6

Dixon hoped the guide would bring some chocolate or other sweets. This is one thing he missed living on the Ticonderoga. He waited a week and then two. The guide never arrived. Dixon was disappointed and angry.

He had paid the guide well when he brought his last delivery. Where was he? He decided to remain one more week. He was anxious to return to his cabin, but he really wanted—and needed—his supplies.

The guide did not arrive. As Dixon treaded back toward his cabin, he knew he would have to hunt, trap, and fish more than before. *When will I have time to do the things that Chris and I dreamed of,* he wondered?

Dixon had traveled about two miles when he thought he heard voices. Stopping in his tracks, he listened. Again, he knew these were human voices. He started walking toward the direction they were coming from. He was on the ridge of a valley and knew the voices could be a mile away. He just hoped they would continue so he could find their location. Suddenly, the voices stopped. Dixon continued in the direction where he imagined the people were. After about an hour, Dixon recognized signs of a camp. A few empty cans were strewn about, and there was a small pile of wood ready for use.

He looked around and could tell that two or more people had been there. Then, approximately three hundred feet from the campsite, Dixon swallowed hard. He saw the lifeless body of a man under some brush. Dixon quickly released the safety of his rifle, laid down his belongings, and slid into the crotch of a large tree. He didn't know if any of the voices he'd heard still might be around. He waited. After what seemed like several hours, Dixon realized he was alone. He approached the body. He wanted to look at the face and also find out the cause of death.

The last part of his question was answered immediately. A small thin rope was wrapped around the man's throat. The man appeared to be around his age, was rugged looking, with a beard. He had a large star-shaped scar on his left cheek. Dixon couldn't find anything in the man's pockets.

Dixon had a small shovel with him and decided to bury him and cover him with rocks. It would be the decent thing to do. As he laid the man into the shallow grave, Dixon noticed the man had a slip of white paper in the grip of his hand. Dixon pulled the paper free and turned pale as he read it. It was a map directing the holder to a "location of the Ticonderoga where he would meet a man named Dixon"!

Dixon couldn't believe what he was reading. *Who was this man? How and why would he have my name? Who killed him and why was he murdered?*

Chills ran down Dixon's back. He looked around to survey the hillsides. He could not see any movements of any kind. As he finished with the burial, he noticed that, on the bottom of the right boot of the victim, a chunk of rubber shaped like a letter T was missing, *probably cut on some sharp rock,* he thought. He tried to think what he should do: head back for the cabin or stay and search this area and return in the morning? He wanted to find out more about the dead man with the note that led to him. He decided to stay and search.

When Dixon returned to the campsite in the morning, everything was quiet; nothing had been disturbed. Dixon knew he was one or two miles from the lake where he and the guide were supposed to have met. He figured the dead man and the murderer probably came from that direction. He headed back toward the lake

As he approached the lake, he realized that he must be at least one half to a mile upstream from where he was to meet the guide three weeks before. Then he noticed parts of a boat on shore. He looked at the pieces and immediately realized the boat had been hacked to pieces with an ax. Dixon also noticed one small piece with the number twelve in a circle. It was the same boat the guide had brought Dixon to the Ticonderoga in! He noticed two sets of footprints in the mud close to shore. It was an impression of a right boot with a piece missing shaped like a T. It was the murder victim's boot imprint.

Dixon looked around the area.

The footprints led toward the area where he had found the dead man, but they disappeared shortly. He also found cigarette butts on the ground. As he searched among the many trees in the area, he noticed a large oak tree that would conceal anyone behind it. This area would have clear visibility of the lake. He guessed that someone was watching the boat come across the lake and then dock.

After the boat driver docked, he must have headed inland. The one in hiding followed. After he murdered the boat driver, he must have come back and destroyed the boat. *Why? And what reason?* Dixon wondered. The supplies were of some value but not enough to murder for . . . unless the murderer didn't want the supplies to reach their intended destination.

Dixon, looking at the piece of paper with his name on it that the victim was holding, suddenly gasped. The victim was probably a replacement guide bringing Dixon's supplies to him and had Dixon's name written down. The guide either missed the scheduled meeting place or was misdirected intentionally.

Thoughts again caused Dixon to shudder, *Am I thinking irrationally? Am I losing my senses? Am I correct in my assumptions?* These questions loomed in Dixon's mind. He looked over his shoulder as he packed up and headed toward his cabin.

Dixon had spent several days waiting for the guide and burying a murder victim.

It was late spring, and summer would be arriving soon. He had much to ponder, on his way back to his "home".

He took advantage of the warm summer, chopping wood, rebuilding his cabin, fishing and hunting.

Chapter 7

It was already late July; fall would begin the first part of September. Dixon picked berries, found wild apple trees, pulled edible plants, and chopped wood every day.

One bright warm August morning, Dixon decided he would pack his gear, take his maps, and explore the Ticonderoga. This would be his first planned exploration. He decided to just go for it. He hoped he would be able to locate the starting point landmark if he was looking for it.

From his cabin, Dixon headed due east. He hiked across parts of the Ticonderoga he had never seen before. One of the marks on the map looked like a rock foundation in the shape of a broken arrow, with the arrowhead pointing to three mountain tops. Dixon determined that if he found the arrowhead location, the mountains would be within two or three miles.

After one week of going east and no sign of any landmarks as indicated on the map, Dixon went north approximately half a mile and then back west toward his cabin. He calculated it would take him at least two to three weeks to complete this cycle. It would require at least eight cycles to completely cover the land that circled his cabin. That would mean up to twenty-four weeks of actual travel time, not counting the time he would need to supply himself and his cabin. The warm weeks of spring until the last days of fall lasted only about twelve weeks in the Ticonderoga. This would mean it would require two good years of ideal conditions, just to completely explore a four-mile radius of his cabin. *This is what I came for*, he thought.

Again his thoughts turned to Chris. Even with the rigorous demands of this type of life, Chris would have loved it. She loved to camp out and hike. Chris loved nature. These thoughts were keeping Dixon strong and determined. He needed to find the mystery of the maps that had caused the death of someone he loved so dearly.

On his way back to his cabin, he saw many signs of impending fall and winter. Squirrels were burying nuts, and rutting season had begun for the deer. He spotted several bears fattening up for their winter hibernation. Dixon climbed trees, searched rocky areas, and hiked around valleys. He was unable to locate any signs that resembled the marks on the maps.

Five weeks from when he left his cabin, he was glad to be back. He knew he didn't have time to rest. He must hunt for his winter meats as cold weather was due. Dixon had learned much from his first winter. He wanted a better one. He had collected fist-sized stones all summer. He built a stone wall around his stove to prevent a reoccurrence of fire from over-heated walls. He dug a second pit to bury berries and fruits. He cut off thick, pine branches to put around the base and on the roof of his cabin. He gathered walnuts to supplement his protein needs.

He continued to track his days on the calendar the boatman had given him. He knew Thanksgiving Day was approaching. The snowfall was unusually light for November, and Dixon took advantage of this mild weather. He would hunt every day for fresh meat. Two days before Thanksgiving, he spotted a group of wild turkeys. One of these was to be his Thanksgiving dinner.

December turned very cold. As New Year's Eve was approaching, Dixon reflected back to his cabin fire one year ago. *This has been a better winter already*, he thought.

The winter months slipped by without incident. Dixon read books, kept the fire burning, and looked forward to spring.

Chapter 8

March came in unusually warm, though the ground would remain frozen for a good month, if not two. Dixon knew there was plenty of winter and cold weather left. *Maybe I should take advantage of this warm spell,* he thought. He decided to travel only a short distance from his cabin and camp out one or two nights. He would pack light. He hoped to find rabbit and deer to supplement his needs and bring the meat back to the cabin.

The lighter he packed, the more food he could carry. The morning he left the cabin, the sun was shining on the snow-covered ground. Dixon knew of an area where he had hunted last fall where he had been successful. It was about four hours northeast of his cabin. As he hiked toward his destination, the sun and snow were exhilarating. He only wished that Chris was with him. *This must be the most beautiful place in the world,* Dixon thought. He arrived at his destination around noon. He put up his tent and gathered some firewood. He knew he had about three hours of light left to hunt. He found a path that deer had been using. He positioned himself in a tree overlooking the path where he would remain until dark. While watching the deer's path, Dixon was surprised to see a group of six or seven coyotes, beyond the deer's path. Dixon had heard coyotes howl and had seen one or two often, but he had never seen a pack like this.

Maybe they are taking advantage of this warmer weather too, Dixon thought. *They probably have scared all the deer away.* By sundown, there were still not any deer to be seen. Dixon returned to his tent and built a fire. He heated some beans and added some rabbit that he had brought with him. "Tomorrow will be better," Dixon said to himself. He would keep the fire burning all night. His body clock woke him every two hours at night since the cabin fire, and this night would be no different. The first time Dixon awoke, he noticed how extremely quiet the Ticonderoga seemed to be. He added wood to his fire and realized it was much colder than he anticipated. He wrapped himself up and fell back to sleep.

When he woke again, he was shivering; the fire was low, but still burning. *Maybe I didn't pick up enough wood*, Dixon thought. As he left his tent, the cold wind hit his face. The wind had shifted from the south and was now coming from the east. The temperature had dropped to close to zero. Dixon knew that as soon as dawn broke, he should head back to his cabin—he hadn't brought warm enough clothing to stay out in this weather. He added wood to his fire. He knew it was still four or five hours until dawn and his supply of wood wouldn't last that long. The snow provided some light and he decided to find some more limbs and downed trees that he could chop up with his hatchet. He had spotted this downed tree that was close to his camp the day before.

Chapter 9

Dixon was not concerned about his decision. He knew the wood was available. He would keep warm and be back in his cabin by noon the next day. He again noticed the silence that surrounded his campsite. The only noise was made by his boots breaking through the snow as he headed for the downed tree.

The old oak had fallen into a group of pines. Dixon started removing pine branches so he could get closer to the fallen trunk. He reached low to grasp a pine branch when the silence was broken by the sounds of barking and snarling. A large gray coyote jumped out of the brush and grabbed Dixon's left arm. He could feel the warm blood running down his hand.

The animal lunged again, and Dixon's hatchet met the coyote's face. His blow knocked the coyote back, but it lunged again. Dixon picked up a pine branch and stuck the end into the animal's wide-open mouth. This time, the coyote reeled back, noticeably injured by Dixon's action.

Dixon had not brought his rifle with him to cut wood. The only weapon he had was his hatchet. He struck at the animal again, but it was too quick and Dixon missed. The animal stared at Dixon but did not attack again. Dixon grasped his arm to slow down the loss of blood. He watched as the animal circled him. He had his hatchet ready. Then to Dixon's amazement, the coyote began walking away. He couldn't see the animal anymore. Dixon's only thought was getting back to his campsite and his rifle. He was afraid the animal would return.

His arm was torn open. He laid his rifle on his lap as he applied pressure to his wound using his hankerchief as a patch. He still needed wood to last until dawn. He returned to the fallen tree, thrashing and making noises as he walked. With his good arm, he was able to chop and carry wood. The morning was cold and Dixon was anxious to start back to his cabin. His arm had a deep gash six inches long. It needed cleansing. Dixon had not brought his first-aid kit for this short trip.

Although he had lost blood, he felt strong enough to walk. He knew if he stayed there, the coyotes would smell blood and return. He had only one choice, and that was to start back. The closer he got to his cabin, the colder it got. The coldness numbed his sore arm. When he arrived at his cabin, he was weak. He had not eaten anything, and he was exhausted. "First things first," he said to himself. "I must build a fire, get something to eat, and clean my wounds, before I crash out.

* * *

The embers were still red when Dixon woke up. It was dark outside, and his arm was throbbing. He built up the fire and fixed soup. He knew his arm required more attention. He cleansed it again and could see muscle and bone. His arm needed stitching to hold the wound together to heal. He got the needle he used to repair the tent with. He would use the lightest test-weight fishing line he had. He had to do it.

Dixon was not a drinking man, but he had brought the fifth of Jack Daniel's that he and Chris had received as a Christmas gift many years before. It had never been opened. He brought the bottle down from the shelf and tears flooded his eyes. He remembered the Christmas like it was yesterday. Chris was asking, "What are we going to do with this?" Now, Dixon would be using it to relax his mind and body to make the repairs on his arm more bearable. Dixon drank the Jack Daniel's and poured some on his wound. He sewed it together without passing out.

Chapter 10

March went into April and the south winds would soon be bringing warmer weather. Dixon's arm was not healing. He was still cleansing the outside, but the pain inside his arm was almost unbearable. He realized that it must be infected. Each time he tried to penetrate the wound to cleanse or drain it, the excruciating pain would almost cause him to black out. He needed medical assistance to save his arm. As each day passed, Dixon became more concerned about it.

Without a guide scheduled to meet him, would he have to amputate his own arm or die an agonizing death from his own body poisoning?

Dixon stepped out of his cabin and for the first time since his arrival at the Ticonderoga, three years prior, he could hear a motor running. Then it appeared, a single engine red-and-white piper with runners that could land in water. Dixon couldn't believe his eyes. The plane was flying low and appeared to be searching the ground. Dixon, waved with his good arm, but the plane passed over without acknowledgment. Dixon ran into his cabin and brought out whatever he could grab with a bright color: a red wool scarf, a yellow cushion, striped socks, a Baltimore Orioles T-shirt. He spread them on the ground. Within minutes, he could hear the motor again. They were coming back, but on this pass they had shifted to the south of Dixon's cabin. It was clear they were on a search mission.

As they made the second pass, Dixon held his breath. Could they possibly have seen his bright clothing lying on the ground? Just as the plane was disappearing over the treetops, he saw it banking to the left. It was turning around! This time, they flew lower, and Dixon could see the pilot inside waving.

The plane circled again. On this pass, he could see two occupants in the plane. The one who was not piloting pointed to himself and then to the direction of the lake. Dixon knew they were going to land in the lake.

He picked up his gear and started the six-mile trek toward the lake. He knew this hike would take him twelve to fourteen hours and he hoped they would wait. Even with his aching arm, Dixon was making good time. He was excited, but also concerned: who were these people, and what were they searching for? They had located his cabin, and as far as Dixon knew, they were the only ones who had even seen it. Regardless, he thought he would soon find the answers to his questions.

Dixon anticipated he would arrive at his regular camping site that he used at the halfway mark of his journey by night fall. But in his excitement, he traveled faster than usual. The sun was still up when he arrived at the site. He decided he would stop anyway, as he was familiar with the area. He set up his tent and started a fire. Suddenly he heard the sounds of something coming through the woods. He grabbed his rifle and waited.

The two men appeared and stopped quickly when they saw his campsite. Dixon recognized the red sweatshirt on one of the men as one of the airplane occupants. He stepped out to greet them. They had decided to leave the airplane and hike toward the cabin. They realized it would take several hours for Dixon to reach the lake, and they hoped to meet him halfway.

Daniel and Cody introduced themselves, explaining they'd been hired by a man named Zach, a former guide for the Ticonderoga area, and his sister, Dessie. The story was that three years ago, Zach had brought a "man named Dixon" to the Ticonderoga to hunt and fish. In the fall, Zach returned to bring supplies and agreed to meet Dixon in the spring. But during the winter, Zach had a heart attack. Zach's sister Dessie was married to another guide, a man named Luke. Luke was not as familiar with the Ticonderoga as his brother-in-law, but Zach told him about his scheduled meeting with Dixon in the spring, and Luke agreed to help him out. Zach had given him written directions of the meeting place and also Dixon's name, but Luke never returned home. Zach and Dessie had hired Daniel and Cody to search the Ticonderoga for *any* signs of life.

At this point, Dixon introduced himself. Daniel and Cody were in disbelief. This was their first flyover of the Ticonderoga. They had mounted extra fuel tanks on their plane in order to complete a round trip. They hadn't expected to locate anything on this first flight.

Dixon showed them his arm and they agreed to fly him to civilization to get medical attention. As soon as day broke they were on their way to the lake. At this point, Dixon didn't know whether to tell them of his discovery of a body or any of the details. He decided he would fill them in later.

Chapter 11

The airplane lifted off the lake, and Dixon looked back over the Ticonderoga. "I will be back," he said to himself.

It took the small plane five hours to arrive at Shaloh, a small Canadian village near Lake Champlain.

The sun was setting as they landed. Cody docked the plane. Their jeep was in the lot, and they took Dixon to a small doctor's office.

He shook his head as he examined Dixon's arm. The arm might be saved if Dixon could get to a surgeon and a hospital. He gave Dixon some pain pills and antibiotics; Cody said he could rent another plane and fly Dixon to Windsor.

The doctor said he would call ahead and make arrangements with a surgeon in Windsor General Hospital, where facilities would be available. They would leave in the morning. Now he would have time to talk to Zach and Dessie. Cody called Zach and said they would be there soon. Dessie would be there too.

Dixon thought about how the news of Chris had struck him, and now he would have to inform them of what he had found in the brush. Disbelief, anguish, heartbreak, and anger. Now he must tell another person of the death of her mate. Her feelings would be similar. Dixon already felt sorrow for Dessie and Zach as he rumbled across town in the cold jeep.

Zach lived in a small house next to the lake, just out of town. The old house needed paint, and a junk car sat in the lane. Zach greeted them at the door. He didn't look anything like the guide who had taken Dixon to the Ticonderoga. This man was graying and thin. He shuffled his feet as he walked. The heart attack had taken its toll. Zach stared at Dixon. They exchanged greetings and reintroductions, and then Zach recognized Dixon. They hugged.

Zach exclaimed, "I didn't think I'd ever see this man again!"

Dessie was sitting in an old wicker rocker clutching a picture frame.

Zach took the picture from her and handed it to Dixon. "Did my brother-in-law ever find you?" he asked.

Dixon looked at the picture of Luke, which showed a man with a star-shaped scar on his left cheek. Dixon sat down to Zack, Dessie and Cody. He told them as he was returning to his cabin from the lake: about the voices he heard and then the discovery of Luke. All four of them were in tears of emotion and relief. They talked late into the night, Dixon told Zach that he was going back as soon as his arm healed. Zach said he didn't know of another guide that could deliver supplies to Dixon.

Cody spoke up. "I can bring food and supplies in my airplane. It'll cost you more, but you'll know when I'm coming, and I can come more often, if you want."

Dixon welcomed the offer.

Cody asked Dixon to spend the night with his family, since they would be leaving early in the morning for Windsor. He agreed and they left Zach's house at midnight. Zach and Dessie had heavy hearts, but they felt a relief just to know where Luke was.

The next day, when they parted at Windsor's airport, Cody made arrangements for someone to call him when Dixon's surgery was over. He told Dixon to let him know when he was ready to return and he would pick him up.

Dixon thanked his new friend and called a taxi to take him to Windsor General Hospital. At ten AM, a Dr. Frazier examined Dixon's arm. Not surprisingly, he found gangrene. "We're going to have to open this arm this afternoon," he said, re-bandaging Dixon's arm. "Your pain level must be high. Gangrene is a late stage of infection and it refers to the dead and dying flesh around a wound . . . if we do not open this immediately you will probably lose your arm.

*   *   *

Dixon stayed two days in Windsor General Hospital. Dr Frazier completey removed all the gangrene, and cleaned the wound thoroughly. Dr. Frazier said the operation was completely successful and that Dixon's strength and range of motion should return to normal. This would require therapy and exercise after the stitches were removed. He told Dixon to return in two weeks to take out the stitches, and then he would require at least two weeks more of therapy.

Dixon caught the next flight to Baltimore. When he arrived, he rented a car and headed to his Cape Cod home in Dovel. He knew it would probably be rented out, but he felt a special feeling in his heart and wanted to see the home that he and Chris had loved so much.

There were cars in the driveway. *Probably college kids having a party*, he thought. Then he drove around the block to the front of Tara's house. Just as he was approaching Tara's driveway, a car was coming from the other direction and started to pull into it. Tara was driving and as she saw Dixon ahead of her, she almost crashed into her house. She couldn't believe her eyes! Dixon got out, and they stood there and gaped at each other in the street. They hugged each other—he with his one good arm, the other being in a sling—and looked again. Tara's expression was confusion and happiness.

"Oh Dixon," she shouted, "I thought you were dead!"

"Dead? Why would you think that?"

"It's been three years, and you said you would contact me—you never did!" she replied. "I didn't know where to begin looking for you."

"It's a long story, Tara. Let's talk over dinner."

"Where are you staying?"

"I just arrived in town, and this is the first place I've stopped. I guess I'll stay at the Amerisuites," Dixon replied.

"Oh no, you won't," she insisted. "You will stay right here. I have four bedrooms, and I can only use one at a time. We have a lot to talk about. Your arm, for example," she said, pointing at his wrapped limb with her eyes.

It had been a long time since Dixon had been in Tara's house. He had never been in her house alone with her. Now, he was going to stay overnight. He felt uneasy as he carried his overnight case into the house. Over dinner, they talked about Chris, the ongoing murder investigation, and what had happened to them in the last three years. Tara said Ted Hands still had no suspect. There were no fingerprints to be found. The way the intruders got into the house was still not known. There was no indication of forced entry.

Ted had told Tara if she ever heard from Dixon, to contact him. She would call him in the morning. "Now, what about you? Where did you end up? And how did you get hurt?" she asked, leaning forward on her elbows across the table from him, all eyes and ears.

"I found a place that I plan to stay for a few more years," Dixon said.

"Really? A 'few more years'? I thought you'd come back to stay!" she exclaimed.

"I actually thought I would be back within a year, when I left before, Tara." He shook his head, and she could almost imagine what he was feeling. He took a breath and pushed the bad memories away. "It was almost impossible to contact you, and I wasn't worried about the house or anything else back here . . . I've actually enjoyed my new way of life. The three years have just passed by."

"Where are you living?" Tara asked. "Can I visit you sometime? I mean, we need to keep in touch! Chris was my—" She couldn't finish that sentence. "Well, there's your house . . ."

In all the years that Chris and Tara were friends, Dixon was never involved in their activities. He was always glad that Chris had Tara as a good neighbor and friend. Now, it seemed to Dixon that Tara considered him to be as close a friend as Chris had been. But they only knew each other secondhand.

"It's a different style of living," Dixon said. "I don't think you would care for it."

"Well, can you tell me what city you're close to? Can I call? Or write to you?" Tara asked.

"Tara," Dixon started, "I don't live near a big city, and I don't have a telephone—it's what you would call…living in the boonies." They stared at each other without a word for a moment. And then Dixon continued, "I promise I'll contact you sooner the next time."

Tara nodded and let him change the subject. They discussed whether to sell Dixon's house or continue to rent it out. They reminisced about Chris. They cried and they laughed.

When Dixon closed his bedroom door, he was wondering why Tara had asked so many questions.

* * *

Dixon was exhausted and slept in late. When he awoke, he could hear voices coming from the kitchen. He took a sponge bath, dressed his arm, and went into the kitchen. Tara and Ted Hands were still talking in low tones as Dixon entered. Ted jumped up to shake Dixon's hand. Ted was still the chief of police. He didn't wear a uniform but was dressed nicely in a turtle neck and sport coat. Tara had evidently filled Ted in with what she and Dixon had talked about.

"Tara tells me you're leaving again," Ted started, "maybe for a few years?"

Dixon was alert to Ted's tone of voice. *Does Ted actually care whether I'm leaving again or is his question because of another reason?* "Yes, I'll be going back in a couple weeks," Dixon replied. "I'm able to enjoy my new life. Is there anything new from your investigation of Chris' death? Tara tells me you've hit a brick wall. It's been three years, Ted. Will you continue your investigation?"

"I plan to solve this murder," Ted replied as he sipped his coffee. Tara poured a cup for Dixon. "What happened to your arm?" Ted asked.

"Oh, I got in a fight with a big dog," said Dixon, "and the dog won. The small-town doctor where I'm living referred me to a specialist, and that's why I'm here now. It's healing well . . . or so the doc says . . . and it will be almost as good as new." He put on his best poker face. He didn't trust either of them, but he couldn't put his finger on why.

"Well, Dixon, if you are enjoying your new location and what you are doing, I don't blame you for wanting to return. Life here is good, but so routine. Since Chris' murder, there has only been one more homicide, and that was a jealous-family situation—already through the courts and a conviction. So . . . where exactly is this *boonie* town, Dixon?"

Wow, Ted's beginning to sound like Tara, Dixon thought. "It's a long way from here, Ted. I don't think you or Mary Jo would want to travel that far."

Ted's face turned red. "Mary Jo and I are divorced. It's been over a year," he said.

"Oh, I'm sorry! I didn't know. Listen, I don't want any particulars . . . I'm just sorry for you and Mary Jo both." Dixon knew Mary Jo from high school. She was a lot like Chris—interested in many things, physically active, sporty, fun-loving. *Whatever happened between Ted and Mary Jo is not my business,* he thought.

"I have some time off coming next year, and traveling a long distance would not bother me," Ted said. "Just let me know where and when—I'll make plans to visit you."

Chapter 12

Dixon was uneasy. He and Ted had been friends for years. They had hunted and fished together. *Now, why does Ted want to know exactly where I live,* he pondered. *We did enjoy doing things together . . .* "Okay, we'll work on that," Dixon said as he searched Ted's eyes. He noticed Ted and Tara glancing at each other as they talked.

"Well," Tara said, "I've got an appointment to show some real estate at eleven o'clock. I'm glad you're here, Dixon. Now, you and Ted enjoy this day. We'll plan dinner tonight with all three of us!"

"Sounds good to me, Tara," Ted replied as he poured coffee into both of their cups.

Dixon agreed, savoring the city-brewed coffee. He'd forgotten how good it could taste. The two men sat in silence as they slugged it back faster than either of them normally would have, the tension between them unacknowledged.

"Dixon, I want to go to my office to review some things with you," Ted murmured as he rinsed the cups and cleaned up the table. "Maybe you can fill in some of the gaps of my investigation."

What more information could I have now than I did three years ago? Dixon thought as they drove across town. They drove by the church that he and Chris had been married in. Memories flooded his mind. *Why?* he wondered. *Chris and I were so happy. Now Ted and Mary Jo are no longer married.*

His thoughts were interrupted by Ted's voice. "When you went through all the papers from your safe, did you find anything,

anything that would help us with our investigation?" the police chief asked.

"No, I don't think so," Dixon lied. "There was around a thousand bucks in cash, our deed, our wills, and our car titles." He did not mention the maps.

"This is what is so strange about this case," Ted continued. "What on earth did they think was in the safe?" He caught Dixon straight in the eye as he asked.

"I wish I knew," Dixon replied, revealing nothing.

When they arrived at Ted's office, he pulled mug shots from his desk drawer. "Look at these, Dixon. Do any of these faces look familiar to you?"

Dixon sorted through many different views of just six males. "No, I don't know any of these dudes, and I don't think I've seen any of them . . . ever," Dixon said, telling the truth. "What's the connection?"

"These are pictures of ex-cons from the Baltimore area. They all have a record of torturing and murdering victims. Believe it or not, two of these slobs were out on bond during the time of Chris' murder. Two had escaped from Maryland's federal penitentiary about the same time. The last two are in custody, charged with the torture and death of an eighty-seven-year-old woman. I wanted you to study these mug shots. Maybe somewhere or sometime before Chris' murder, you might have seen one of them. I know it is a long shot."

But Dixon did not recognize any of them.

Tara had made reservations at Kedro's, an expensive restaurant in Baltimore. It wasn't the cost that bothered Dixon, but the atmosphere, the dress code, and darkness did. He and Chris had visited restaurants like this and enjoyed them, but tonight was different. He thought of the simplicities of his cabin and how much he had changed, and the desire to return to the Ticonderoga increased.

At the end of dinner, Ted was paged on his beeper. He called in and returned to the table. He had to leave immediately because there was an emergency back in Dovel. "I'll call you in the morning,

Tara," he said to her as he was leaving the table, "and I'll probably see *you* some time tomorrow," as he looked at Dixon.

Dixon and Tara arrived home around midnight. Tara turned on the stereo and poured some teas. "I think it would be great if Ted could visit you sometime," she stated. "He needs to get away from his pressures and the politics involved in his position. And as I said before, maybe I could even visit you. Would you like that?" she asked, her eyes never leaving his.

"I don't know, we'll have to see," Dixon stammered. He was surprised at Tara's secretive look as she talked to him. "Are you and Ted dating?" Dixon asked, even while he wondered why he was asking.

"No, we're just good friends," Tara replied. "Ted comes over a lot, and we dine and talk together, but that's about it."

Dixon didn't believe her. *It isn't any of my business,* he thought, but he was spending nights there and he didn't want to interfere with their relationship. He couldn't figure what his problem was. Suspicious of everyone. He wasn't like this . . . before. "I think I'll turn in," he said. "Good night, Tara. Thanks for this—for including me in your life." She smiled sadly, her teacup and her knees tucked under her chin. And then he went to his bedroom.

Although his overnight bag was nearly empty, he noticed it was not where he had left it. He opened the drawers of the dresser he was using and knew his clothing had been rearranged. *Maybe Tara has a cleaning lady,* he considered. He pulled a book from the shelf, turned on the light over his bed, and welcomed the clean sheets and soft mattress.

Engrossed in his fictional mystery, he did not hear the soft tap on his door. Then a louder tap caught his attention. "Yes," Dixon said, "I'm in bed."

Tara slowly opened the door and stood in the doorway. A light from the other room was glowing through her gown.

"What is it, Tara, is something wrong?" Dixon asked.

"I just couldn't sleep," Tara said as she entered the room.

Dixon laid his book down and pulled the covers up to his naked chest. "Maybe you should . . . read a good book too," Dixon stammered. "It helps."

Tara sat down on the edge of Dixon's bed. She put her hand on his hands as she leaned in to kiss him.

"Tara, you were such a good friend of Chris' . . . and for that I am thankful. I also appreciate all you have done for me. You have rented my home, taken care of other business affairs for us . . . for me, and allowed me to stay here. You are also very attractive, and I thank you from my heart for caring for me, but I'm not ready for this." He tried to put the brakes on her gently, but she looked a little dejected as she flinched back. "It's not you, Tara. It's me," he said, hoping she would back off and leave his bedroom right now. "Forgive me?"

Dixon sunk into the headboard with a sigh of relief as Tara left the room and closed the door. He couldn't believe what had just happened! He had always liked Tara as a *friend* and never thought of her any other way. He thought that feeling was mutual and the relationship purely platonic. He turned off his light, pulled on the covers, and dropped off to sleep.

Dixon was up early. He made the coffee and thought about last night's episode. Would Tara speak to him this morning? Would she even get up? His questions were soon answered. Tara greeted Dixon as she poured her coffee. "About last night," Dixon started to speak, "I'm sorry—"

"No, *no!*" Tara said. "I'm the one who's sorry! I just thought our attraction to each other was more than friendship. It was all my fault. Will you forgive me?" Before Dixon could answer, the phone rang. Tara talked to Ted briefly and handed the phone to Dixon.

"I have an extremely busy day, Dixon. Maybe tonight we can get together again," Ted was saying. "How much longer will you be here?"

Dixon glanced at Tara's kitchen calendar. "I'll be here about four more days . . ."

"Let me talk to Tara again," Ted said.

"I'll take it in the den," hummed Tara, "just hang up, will you? When you hear my voice?"

Tara walked into the den, and Dixon hung up the phone.

Chapter 13

He couldn't put it all together. The last few days he noticed the glances and looks that Tara and Ted shared with each other. *Why would Tara come on to me?* he wondered.

Tara came back into the kitchen. "Again, about last night, Dixon, I am sorry."

"Forget it, Tara; it never happened," said Dixon, wishing that were true.

"No, but it did," said Tara, taking him by surprise with her suddenly serious tone. She sat down at the table next to him, took a breath and then the words spilled out. "I have enjoyed being with you since your return. You know I've never had a serious relationship with anyone. I think I'm falling in love with you. I wish you would stay in Dovel. I know you want to return to *the boonies*, as you put it, but we could visit there . . . ?" Tara pleaded.

Dixon was without words. He didn't know anything about her past before he and Chris met her the day they moved into their Cape abutting her backyard. Chris and Tara became close friends, and the three of them enjoyed cookouts, holiday dinners, and the theatre. He didn't even know if Tara was ever married or anything. He and Chris never asked or cared. Now, Tara was telling him she loved him!

"Tara . . ." Dixon searched for the right words, disbelieving this was happening again. No wonder he loved the backwoods. There was none of this nonsense. "You are a beautiful person. I like you very much. You've been very kind and accommodating to me. But I

34

haven't even *thought* about another woman since Chris died. Falling in love with someone else has never entered my mind. I know time will continue to heal my loss, and I suppose loving someone else will happen . . . eventually. But it's just not now. Maybe I should leave today and head back to Windsor. My appointment with the specialist is just a few days from now . . . and I have a regimen of physiotherapy to undergo."

Dixon had not shared with Ted or Tara that the therapy would only be for two weeks. He decided he would stay in Windsor for the duration and then head out.

"Oh, Dixon," Tara cried, "please don't leave! I don't know what came over me. I have only loved one other man in my life, and he is gone. I have never had feelings for anyone else until these sweet days with you. I don't want you to leave at all, but I know I can't force you to love me. Stay here these next few days. I will continue to be a faithful and responsible friend. *Please!*"

"Okay," Dixon replied, "but I will be leaving Thursday morning. I will keep my promise. I will contact you within the next six months. By then my feelings or yours may change. Thank you for sharing your love for me. I am flattered." They embraced and kissed each other on the cheek.

"Ted will be stopping by around seven tonight," Tara said, without missing a beat. Her voice was steady now, without a sign of disappointment. "Have you made a decision about your house? It would bring a good price if you decide to sell, but the demand for rentals is still high."

Keeping the house wouldn't bring Chris back, Dixon thought. *I couldn't live there again anyway.* "Put it on the market," he said, and Tara jotted down notes. "If it sells, just deposit the money into my savings account."

Tara had kept an account for Dixon's rent income and to draw from to pay for any upkeep on the house. "I have an eleven o'clock appointment. I should be home around five o'clock. Ted's bringing some ingredients with him, so we will cook in tonight," she said, like they were just old buds.

Dixon was relieved, and that seemed like a great idea to him too. He was tired of restaurants. "I'll prepare one of my favorite dishes," he said, laughing, as Tara was leaving.

"I'll be looking forward to that," she said as she closed the door, "but no squirrel!" she hollered, laughing as she went.

At eleven-thirty, Tara's phone rang four times until the answering machine came on. Whoever called decided not to leave a message, Dixon figured as the tape whirled. He never answered Tara's phone when he was there alone. He knew the call would be for her and let the answering machine take care of any messages.

He walked to a nearby small grocery store. He wasn't kidding about the cooking; he had become a self-described expert in making soup. He would buy the items, he needed, and his own special ingredients and have the soup ready for dinner. When he returned to Tara's house, the phone was ringing again. And again, there was no message left on the answering machine.

Dixon cleaned his vegetables and was looking for a pot large enough to accommodate the amount of soup he wanted to prepare. The telephone rang again. At the end of the fourth ring, Dixon had the thought that there might be a malfunction with the answering machine, so picked up the phone. "Hello" he started, "Tara isn't here—"

"Dixon?" a female voice inquired. "Is this Dixon?"

"Yes, this is Dixon," he replied, "and who am I speaking with?"

"Is Ted Hands there?" the woman asked.

Dixon hesitated. "May I ask who's calling please?"

"Dixon, this is Mary Jo Hand; Ted isn't there, is he?"

"No, Mary Jo, I am here alone. How are you doing? I'm so sorry to hear about you and Ted," he continued.

"Dixon . . ." Mary Jo sounded frightened. "I must talk to you. I don't want Tara or Ted to know that I've called. I kept hoping you would answer the phone. I don't know what Ted or Tara have told you," Mary Jo said, "I need to meet you soon."

Chapter 14

"I will be leaving in a few days, Mary Jo . . . How did you know I was here?" he asked.

"We can discuss that when we talk," she replied. "Can you meet me tomorrow?"

"Sure," Dixon replied. "What would be a convenient place and time?"

"I'll meet you at Harold's Pantry on Wilson Drive so we can talk. Dixon, this is important. If Ted knew I called you, I don't know what he would do."

"I won't say a word," Dixon replied as he was hanging up the phone.

He thought of Mary Jo's quivering and frightened voice as he began cleaning up the mess he had made on the countertop. *What could be so important for her to talk to me in such a secretive manner?* He found a large stockpot. Now he was ready to complete his soup specialty for dinner.

Tara arrived around five thirty. She'd bought three large steaks from the local butcher. "Ted will be bringing his homemade baked bread. He's got a new one of those bread machines," she said as she emptied her sack. "We should start the grill at six thirty. It will take these big potatoes a while to get completely baked. Where is your favorite dish?" she asked.

"It's cooking on the stove and almost ready to eat," Dixon said.

Ted arrived at seven o'clock.

Each one raved about the others' specialties. After they finished and cleaned up, they settled down in the den. Tara was excited about selling a beautiful home in an affluent neighborhood in Baltimore. Ted's day sounded busy and complicated. Dixon wondered what tomorrow would bring.

"I've got the dimensions of your house and lot," Tara said, looking at Dixon. "We'll prepare a listing tomorrow and have you look it over. I've got some ideas on price but will need your input. Could you come by my office around noon?" she asked. Dixon searched for an answer. "I have plans after lunch," he finally said. "I can meet with you at ten or ten thirty."

"I'll need to shift an appointment," Tara replied. "That won't be a problem; ten thirty will be fine.

"What time will you be leaving for Windsor?" Ted asked. "I've got time to take you to the airport in Baltimore."

Dixon almost dropped his coffee. He knew he had mentioned Windsor to Tara but no one else. *How did Ted find out where I am going?* he wondered. "The car rental is next to the airport. I'll be taking it back anyway," Dixon said. "Thanks for the offer."

The three of them did the dishes and kitchen clean up together, and then Ted left at eleven PM. Dixon and Tara chatted some more.

"It sounds like Ted was overwhelmed with work today," Dixon stated. "It's a good thing you and he made plans for tonight's dinner when you talked this morning."

"Oh yes," Tara said, "I never call him at his office during the day unless it's important." She yawned and then Dixon did the same. They laughed. "Yawning is so contagious," Tara said.

Dixon stood and moved toward his bedroom. "We better retire for the night, Tara. See you in the morning," he said and closed his door and climbed in bed without even washing up. He picked up his book, turned on his bed lamp, and pulled up the sheets. But he didn't open his book. His mind was on Ted. *If Tara did not call him, how did he know I was going to Windsor? Is Tara telling me the truth about not calling him?* The urgency and tone of Mary Jo's voice entered his thoughts. It seemed like a short, restless night when Dixon awoke at seven AM.

Tara and Dixon arrived in the kitchen at the same time. They exchanged greetings and briefly discussed the great meal served last evening. Tara was leaving for her office. "I'll see you at ten thirty," she said as she shut the door behind her.

Chapter 15

I t was a beautiful, warm June day in Dovel. Dixon was reminded of the short summer in the Ticonderoga. *Cool weather would be arriving there by the first of August,* he thought as he drove to Tara's office. His arm was healing, and he would be back in time to chop wood and prepare for winter.

Tara was an efficient real-estate broker. She had photos and listings and prices of homes that sold in the last twelve months in the area around their homes. They reviewed the features of his property and agreed upon a price and terms. Dixon signed the real-estate contract. "I'll be home around five," she said as Dixon started for the door. "Will you be there?"

"I believe I will," Dixon unwaveringly replied. "If I am going to be much later, I'll call you."

Dixon arrived at Harold's Pantry at five minutes before twelve. He could see Mary Jo sitting at the table near the windows. She was watching for him and managed a weak smile as he got out of his car and waved at her.

Mary Jo was a pretty woman who was a sharp dresser. She had worked at a fitness club when Dixon left Dovel three years ago. Everyone enjoyed being around Mary Jo, with her high-pitched laugh and her sparkling green eyes. She loved children, but she and Ted had never become parents.

When Dixon approached, Mary Jo rose and grasped his hand. "I'm so glad you could come," she stated. "I wanted to talk to you." She couldn't keep back the tears.]

Dixon noticed small lines in Mary Jo's forehead. Her eyes looked tired and worried. She was thinner than Dixon had remembered. He squeezed her hand again to reassure her that he was there for her. "Shall we have a bite to eat?" Dixon asked.

"I'm not hungry, but I'm sure you are," she replied. "I'll have a salad. We can't talk here," she continued without a breath. "You don't mind going to my apartment, do you? It's only two miles from here."

"No, I don't mind," Dixon found himself saying, though he was famished. He couldn't deny it was quite noisy in Harold's Pantry. "Let's get it to go. My treat."

Mary Jo ordered a salad and Dixon took the special. He could tell that she was anxious to leave and suggested he meet her at home.

"I'm driving that white Cavalier over there," she said, pointing out the plate-glass window. "I'll wait in the car, and then you can just follow me. It won't take long to get there."

"Okay, that'll work," he said, getting anxious from her anxiety. He felt calmer as soon as she went to wait in her car. When he got the order, he took the paper sack to his rental, and waved that he was ready. She pulled out faster than you could say, "Follow that car," but he managed to keep up.

Mary Jo's apartment was in a large, old two-story colonial-style house. She led him to the second floor. "Would you like some ice tea?" she asked, and he accepted.

He looked around the room. There were no pictures of anyone. The curtains were closed. It felt like they were isolated from the outside world. *This would be a depressing place to live,* he thought.

Mary Jo brought the tea in, put it on the coffee table, and sat down across from him. "Well, Dixon, the first question I need to ask," she began, "is what have Tara or Ted told you about myself or the divorce?"

Dixon thought for a moment and replied, "A few days ago, when Ted and I were talking and I mentioned your name, he told me you were divorced. I consider all of you my friends and told Ted I didn't need to know the particulars and that I was sorry, for both your sakes. That's it. It was never mentioned again by Ted or Tara. In fact, we have not talked about you at all."

"Dixon, you do need to know some of the particulars," she replied, "because you are involved in them. That's why I wanted to talk to you."

"How am I involved?" Dixon inquired, shocked by the accusation. "I wasn't even here! Are you telling me your divorce was partly caused by something I did? How could that be?"

"I'll start from the beginning," Mary Jo said. She picked up a book that appeared to be a diary. "Dixon," she said, looking him in the eyes, "if Ted or Tara find out that you and I have met, they will be furious. I'm afraid of what Ted might do. They would deny some the things I'm going to share with you. I've kept dates, times, and places in this book. Ted and Tara have been discussing you. I didn't understand at first what they were discussing, but I think it's important for you to know. I'm trusting you, Dixon. What I did hear . . . I have not shared this information with anyone else."

By now, Dixon was sitting on the edge of his chair. *What is all of this about?* he wondered.

"After Chris' murder," she began, "Ted spent a lot of time at your house and in your neighborhood. He told me it was going to take a long time to solve. After you left, he continued to visit there every week. He told me he didn't want to give up. One day, upon leaving an appointment I had in that area, I drove by Tara's house, and Ted's blazer was in her driveway. I didn't think too much about it as I knew how close Tara and Chris were, and with Tara's backyard connected to yours, I figured Ted was seeking answers." Mary Jo picked up her ice tea to take a moment, and Dixon did too. But they just put their glasses back down again, without even taking a sip.

"I asked Ted that night if he had learned anything new concerning the murder. He became angry. He said the investigation was at a dead end and that he had not been involved in it for the last two weeks. He had turned it over to the Detective Division.

"I was surprised—shocked really—by his response, but I never came out and told him what I'd seen that day. As the next few weeks went by, Ted became more and more withdrawn from me. When I said something about it, he would just get angry and storm out."

Neither of them had touched their tea. Mary Jo was shaking and started to cry.

"One afternoon, after he just left. I had an eye appointment—at my specialist on the south side. Ted wasn't interested in my life, so he was unaware where I would be traveling that day. On the way to my appointment, I noticed Ted's Blazer—with the red and blue lights on the dash, it's easy to spot—at a restaurant. I turned around and went back. I walked in, hoping to sit down with him and talk . . . about *us*.

"I could see him at a booth with his back to me. He was sitting with Tara. They were side by side, so neither of them noticed me as I sat down at a table on the other side of a planter. I could just make out what they were saying—I wrote down what I could hear. Ted was saying something about *the CIA* and *the FBI*. Then I heard him talk about an *undercover agent* and some extremely valuable papers that they *surmised that Chris' husband was in possession of*. Ted told Tara, 'We must get those papers. When you hear from Dixon, notify me immediately. This is *big time*, Tara,' he said." At this point, Mary Jo was crying, "And then he said to Tara, 'I love you so much!'" Mary Jo couldn't talk anymore. She got up to walk around and found some Kleenex.

"I could not believe what I was hearing! I wanted to scream, I wanted to tear her eyes out. And his. I couldn't move," she continued. Then she slumped down in her chair.

Dixon leaned back into his seat. He didn't say a word for a few minutes. His mind was dashing back and forth. Everything that happened since his return to Dovel had become a mystery. But Ted and Tara were his friends! Or were they? Tara had said that she and Ted were just friends, and then she had tried to seduce Dixon. *Now Mary Jo is telling me they are lovers!*

Mary Jo started talking again. This time, her voice was subdued and hesitant. "I told . . . Ted . . . about seeing his car . . . at Tara's . . . and that I had seen him . . . with Tara . . . in the restaurant. He went crazy. At first he denied that anything was between him and Tara. He said he still wanted to solve Chris' murder and Tara was helping him. Then I told him I heard him tell Tara that he loved her. Ted hit the wall! 'You were spying on me? What else do you think you heard?' I told him. 'I've heard enough; you can't stay here tonight,'" Mary Jo recalled.

Chapter 16

"'I 'll see you in court!' he yelled as he slammed the door. Needless to say, Dixon, I had a sleepless night. Then he returned the next morning," she continued, "and he stormed into our house, went into the bedroom, and started packing his clothes. He yelled and cursed at me. He said I was psychotic and needed to see a psychiatrist. 'I don't ever want to see you in Tara's neighborhood,' he yelled. 'When Dixon comes back to town, you stay away from him. It's none of your business!'" Mary Jo tried to conceal the hurt. "We never attempted to reconcile our marriage. I knew it was over on that day." Mary Jo sat and stared with tears dropping off her cheek.

"I don't know what to say, Mary Jo, I'm sorry," Dixon said as he stood up. "This whole thing is crazy. I believe I know which papers they were talking about, but I don't know how they even knew I had them."

"I'm not blaming you, Dixon," Mary Jo replied. "I just wanted you to know what happened. Where do I go from here?" she asked.

"Are you still working at the fitness club?" Dixon asked as he sat down again to face her.

"Only part-time, three nights a week. I work full-time at the hospital now. I needed the money, and I wanted to keep busy," she replied.

"I'm planning on leaving Thursday," Dixon began. "I would like to find out more about what Ted and Tara are really up to, but

I'm sure I can't put it all together in the next two days. I will not discuss this conversation you and I had today with anyone. And I suggest you stay away from their part of town. I would like to have your telephone numbers at the hospital and at home. I will call you when I can."

"Can I call you?" Mary Jo asked.

"Where I am staying, there is no telephone available," Dixon replied. "But I will get you a number to call if you want to get in touch with me. If you do call this number, it will take me at least two or three days to return your call." Dixon had not asked Cody for his telephone number, but he knew he would be willing to be a contact if needed. "I must go," Dixon continued. "I'm glad you called me. I'll be at Tara's tonight, but I'll keep one eye open." He smiled. They stood up and hugged each other. Mary Jo clung on, not wanting Dixon to leave. Finally, she released her grip.

Dixon felt sorrow for Mary Jo as he drove away. Her sincerity was convincing.

I'm glad neither Ted nor Tara know I have to stay in Windsor for maybe two more weeks for therapy, he thought. *From what Mary Jo had told him, those two think I have some valuable papers. The only papers I have are the maps. How could either one of them know about these papers? Would Chris have told Tara about them?* Dixon wondered. *If she did, it would have been an innocent statement to Tara. These maps must contain information leading to something much larger than I ever thought. Could Ted be serious in his statement to Tara about the FBI and the CIA?*

Dixon only knew Chris' grandfather a brief period of time. When he met Chris, her grandfather was still working for the government. His wife of forty years had died of cancer. His office was in the Pentagon, and he was friends with many members of the Senate and the House. One of his last trips overseas was to Israel. When he returned, Chris visited him in Washington, DC.

When she returned to Dovel, she told Dixon that her grandfather had changed. Always a jovial, happy man, he appeared sad and concerned. He had told Chris he was going to retire at the end of the year. "I know he's over sixty-five years old, but he always said he would never retire," Chris had said. And then he was killed by a hit-and-run driver just one month after he retired.

Dixon looked at the clock on his dash as he drove into Tara's lane. It was exactly five thirty. Ted's Blazer was parked in the driveway.

The weather had turned warm. Ted and Tara were on the back patio talking and drinking colas. The three of them exchanged greetings. "Your home will be listed in our next MLS listings due out in about ten days," Tara said. "I took pictures of the house this afternoon. I also talked to the renters to let them know. They appeared interested in purchasing the home themselves, but they are unsure of their ability to finance. I don't think it will be on the market long," she continued. "It's a lovely home, and we have it priced fairly."

"I hope it does sell fast," Dixon replied. "Since I've been gone three years, I have no desire to go back in it." Dixon was feeling uneasy. He went into the house to get a cola. He looked out the patio door at Tara and Ted and thought about Mary Jo's conversation with him. *I've got to get back to the Ticonderoga before fall*, he thought. There would be time to explore another section before winter.

Chapter 17

He went to his bedroom and called the airline that would take him to Windsor from Baltimore. "Is there a flight available tomorrow to Windsor?" he asked. "I have reservations for Thursday but would like to change them if possible."

The reservations attendant found a seat on a flight that was going out at ten thirty AM.

"Fine, I will take it," Dixon replied.

Dixon's head was spinning. *Why is all of this happening?* he thought. *First, I fall in love with Chris; then Chris' untimely and tragic murder . . . I return home to chaos and Tara's advances, Ted and Mary Jo's divorce . . . I have to get out of here. Thank goodness my arm is healing well. As soon as the stitches are removed, I'll go back to the Ticonderoga. I can perform the therapy needed myself.*

When he returned to the patio, Ted had started the grill. "We're going to throw on some hamburgers," he stated, "and Tara's tossing up a salad."

"Sounds good to me," Dixon replied. He went into the kitchen to help Tara.

"Did you make your appointment today in time?" she asked.

"Yeah," Dixon replied, wondering if the question was just conversation or was Tara hoping for a more definite answer. "I had lunch and visited some friends," he lied. He knew if he said *friend,* Tara would pick up on that and wonder who he had visited with.

"I wish you didn't have to go back so soon," she said. "We have doctors in Baltimore that could remove your stitches, you know— then you could stay longer."

"I appreciate that, Tara, but I do need to get back to get my house ready for winter." He decided not to tell Tara or Ted about his decision to leave in the morning.

"If you could," Ted started, "call me at least once a month. If something would break in Chris' murder, I would need to talk to you."

"Okay, I'll call you when it's possible," Dixon replied, knowing once a month would be impossible.

"I've got another busy day scheduled tomorrow," Ted continued. "I must go, see you tomorrow evening."

"I don't think I'll go into my office tomorrow," Tara said. "Since it's your last day here, I thought maybe you and I could enjoy the time together."

"Tara," Dixon replied, "I know how much you hate good-byes. I have made plans to fly out tomorrow morning instead of Thursday. I was going to tell you when you got up."

"Dixon! Why? I was looking forward to being with you all day tomorrow." She got up from her chair and sat down by Dixon. She put both arms around him and kissed him on the lips. Dixon pulled away politely. "I love you, Dixon!" Tara said with tears welling up in her eyes. "I don't want you to leave at all."

"We discussed this before, Tara," Dixon replied, searching for words he couldn't find. "I must go to my room and pack. I'll be leaving early; please don't tell Ted that I'm leaving. I'll call him soon." Dixon hugged Tara. "Thank you for everything you've done for me. I will call you . . . as I promised. See you around six thirty in the morning. Good night, Tara."

Packing his clothes, Dixon thought about the things Mary Jo had told him. If Ted and Tara were lovers, you couldn't tell it while being with them. Dixon was confused. Was Tara's love for him real as she indicated or was she using his feelings to induce information from him, but what about Mary Jo? Her look of despair and her sadness were so evident. The details she gave of Ted and Tara's conversation surely were not concocted to justify a divorce.

On his last night in Dovel, he was restless.

Chapter 18

When Dixon awoke, he could smell coffee brewing. Tara was already up. He dressed, closed his suitcase, and carried it into the kitchen with him. "I couldn't sleep," Tara said as she was pouring two cups of coffee. "My heart is heavy. It's hard to believe you're leaving. It seems like it was just yesterday when you arrived," she said as she managed a smile.

"Would you like some toast?" she asked as she was already putting the bread into the toaster.

"Yes," Dixon replied. "I am going to miss all of these conveniences. I'll be leaving in about an hour," he continued. "My flight to Windsor is out at ten-thirty." They sipped coffee, and neither one talked for a few minutes.

"I don't want you to wait six months to contact me," Tara said. "Will you promise to call me within a month?" she asked with tears welling in her eyes. "I'm really going to miss you!"

Dixon quickly analyzed his timeframe. *I'll be arriving at the Ticonderoga the first part of July, I could take plenty of supplies enabling me to have more time to hunt and chop wood. I do want to talk to Mary Jo again before fall. Cody could pick me up in August before cold weather settled in.* "I will call you sometime in August," Dixon said.

"I'll be waiting!" she exclaimed. "I don't know how I'm going to explain this to Ted," Tara said as Dixon was loading his rental.

"Just tell him the truth," Dixon said. "That I didn't tell you until late last night that I was leaving today, and I asked you not to call him."

"I'll call him in August after I call you." This seemed to pacify her.

"One more kiss before you go," she said as she hugged him. You be careful!" she shouted as he drove away.

Dixon arrived at the airport in Baltimore with plenty of time to call Cody. He wanted Cody to meet him at the Windsor airport Friday morning. *This would give me all day Thursday to have the stitches removed and some therapy work started*, he thought. He called Dr. Frazier's office and made the arrangements.

* * *

"Your arm has healed almost completely," Dr. Frazier began as he removed the stitches and examined the wound. "But you'll need more than my initial estimate of two weeks of physiotherapy. I do think with four to six weeks, though, it will be good as new."

"Dr. Frazier," Dixon said, "where I am living . . . it requires a lot of physical work. I'll be using my arms every day. If the physical therapist can instruct me, give me some exercises that I can perform myself, and tell me how not to overdo it . . . I prefer to pass on the four to six weeks of therapy. I need to return home tomorrow."

"It's your arm," Dr. Frazier replied, swallowing his disappointment in his patient's attitude, "and I can't force you to stay. I'll inform the physical therapist to instruct you on proper procedure of exercising. Good luck," he said as he left the room.

Cody met him in Windsor as promised, and they began their long flight to Shaloh. "Zach had another heart attack when you were gone," Cody said, "but he didn't survive this one. We buried him last week."

"That's too bad," Dixon replied. "He was an excellent guide, and a good person."

"There are fewer and fewer guides left in the Shaloh area," Cody continued. "This plane cannot be maneuvered where many hunters want to be dropped off. You were the first and only one I have flown into that part of the Ticonderoga. I don't know of any other planes equipped to fly roundtrip that far from Shaloh."

Dixon asked him about a pickup in late August for an overnight stay in Shaloh. Cody agreed.

Chapter 19

"We know there was another person involved in Luke's death," Dixon said. "So . . . who brought *that* person to the Ticonderoga?"

"I've been thinking about that too," Cody replied. "I talked to all the guides in Shaloh. None of them took anyone near that part of the Ticonderoga. Most guides won't travel that far. Zach was one of a kind. He sure felt bad that he asked Luke to help him when everything ended like it did."

"Have you talked to Air Traffic Control at Shaloh about any planes that have landed in the last year that might have been equipped to fly deep into the Ticonderoga?" asked Dixon.

"Air Traffic Control is pretty tight-lipped," Cody said, "but I do have a friend who works for them. We'll do some checking when we get back."

It was late afternoon when they arrived at Shaloh. They would spend a couple of nights at Cody's before flying on to the Ticonderoga. The next morning, Dixon was awakened by a loud clap of thunder. It was pouring rain and cool for July.

Cody's wife, Linda, was preparing breakfast, and Cody was on the phone. She poured Dixon a cup of coffee. Cody hung up and appeared excited as he pulled out a chair and sat down. "I just talked to Jerry—he's the friend I told you about who is an air traffic controller at the airport. He's off work today. He wants you and me to come over to his house. He has some interesting information . . ."

Jerry lived on the north side of Shaloh. Some of the nicest homes in town were located in this area. Cody did not share with Dixon the discussion he'd had with the man that morning. Jerry opened the garage service door as they drove in. After introductions, Dixon noted a late-model four-wheel-drive truck and a new Acura. It appeared Jerry was successful and perhaps ambitious.

They sat down at the kitchen table and Jerry served coffee.

"Tell Dixon everything you and I discussed this morning," Cody said.

"Let's go into my office," Jerry said as he got up. Cody and Dixon followed. "We keep logs of all incoming and outgoing flights," Jerry stated. "These logs are not confidential but also not public knowledge—only available on a need-to-know basis. I have access to these logs anytime I need to review flight dates or times of aircraft traffic in and out of Shaloh. I just punch it up on the computer. This information is requested by the FAA and the IFFA for different reasons. Since I seem to be the 'computer whiz,' as they call me, I'm on twenty-four-hour call, seven days a week. Luckily, my home computer has access to the modem at the airport. When Cody called this morning asking if any other aircraft had landed in Shaloh equipped to fly into the Ticonderoga, I knew I wanted to talk to you."

He turned to look at one of the many pictures he had lining the walls of his office. These framed glossies showed him standing next to small planes, old planes, new planes, and the one he was indicating: a helicopter. "I started flying helicopters about seven years ago," he continued, "but these helicopters were not large enough or able to fly the distance we're talking about. About six years ago, a large military-type looking helicopter requested permission to land in Shaloh. I was on duty and gave the approval to land. I was excited, as helicopters have always fascinated me, and this would be a first at the airport, except for my small whirlybird."

As Jerry talked, he was punching information into his computer. "This beauty landed," he continued, "and I was surprised to see the pilot was alone. I'll have his name here in a second. His flight plan was to continue to Accordia, about five-hundred miles north of Shaloh. His helicopter was equipped with extra fuel tanks permitting him to fly there and back, although it would be the maximum distance he should attempt. Normally, someone would refuel in Accordia before a return flight.

"Here we go." Jerry hesitated, "His name was Frank Norris."

"Frank Norris?!" Dixon exclaimed.

"Do you know him?" Cody asked.

"Frank Norris was my wife's grandfather," Dixon replied, unable to conceal anxiety and excitement. "What would be in Accordia for him to visit?" Dixon wondered aloud.

"Here's the weird part, Dixon," Jerry said. "Frank Norris never arrived in Accordia. He flew back to Shaloh two days after he left. He still had sufficient fuel left in his tanks, and we assumed he'd filled up in Accordia. He refueled here and his flight plan was to go to Washington, DC, with a stopover in Minneapolis. He was a fine gentleman, very intelligent and appeared young for his white hair. I expressed my interest in helicopters and asked questions about the one he was flying. He just said he worked for the United States government and the copter was one they gave him to fly because the extra fuel tanks would permit him to cover long distances over desolate country. After he left, I discovered Mr. Norris had forgotten to leave the copy of the flight plans *from* Accordia. I called Air Traffic Control in Accordia for this information. To my surprise, Frank Norris had never arrived in Accordia.

"There was no record of him landing *anywhere* within five hundred miles from Shaloh. We contacted ATC in Minneapolis and requested that Mr. Norris leave a copy of his flight plan into Shaloh from Accordia . . . or wherever . . . and to call us when he arrived in Minneapolis. He never contacted us. We are required by the International France Flight Authority (IFFA) to notify the FAA of the United States of circumstances where a pilot of any aircraft does not follow proper protocol. Three days after, an official from the FAA in Washington, DC, contacted the French IFFA. This official apologized for Mr. Norris' lack of communication. The flight in question involved classified information. The completion of this inquiry would be between the two government agencies. In other words," Jerry said, "they told us to butt out. We never saw or heard from Mr. Norris again."

"Frank Norris was my wife's grandfather," Dixon repeated, thinking how blown away Chris would be by this information. "My wife and he were very close . . . He was killed by a hit-and-run driver . . . around six years ago. Then, about two years after he died, my wife was brutally murdered. Frank never told us about his flight here . . . but that wouldn't be unusual as his position in the government did not permit much discussion of his activities. We were never sure whether to believe everything was classified like he said. I guess . . . it was."

"Well, Dixon," Cody said, "your question of the ability of another aircraft capable of flying into the Ticonderoga and back has been answered. It appears like Chris' grandfather might have made that flight."

Dixon knew Cody was right. Frank Norris had influence and powerful friends. If he needed a helicopter, he would have access to one. His position allowed him political immunity in foreign countries, including Canada. He had chosen the Ticonderoga as a location to hide something. After he finished, he made a map of its location. Whether he planned to return to the Ticonderoga or kept the maps for other reasons, Dixon did not know.

"Frank Norris' visit to Shaloh was an inspiration for me," Jerry said. "Ever since that big bird flew out of our airport, I've had a goal to have one someday. I could fly hunters to any part of the Ticonderoga. It would be more expensive than a boat, but think of the travel time saved. Hunters aren't concerned about expense. I know there aren't many boat guides left in Shaloh, and my bird would be available and profitable . . . So, I started writing letters and calling friends of mine in the US. I needed a connection with someone who could help me locate a surplus helicopter that I could rebuild. You two are the first to know, except for my wife, that I am the owner of a helicopter."

"Where are you hiding it?" Cody asked.

"I'm still putting it together," Jerry said. "It came in parts. I bought the old Lemark farm out on Morse Road. It is only twenty acres, but it has a good solid barn. I'll have it completed by spring—with the extra fuel tanks."

Cody was excited too. "Maybe you can teach me how to fly your helicopter."

"With your flying experience, Cody, you could learn quickly. I would want a navigator to assist me, especially over the Ticonderoga," Jerry said.

"That would be great!" Cody exclaimed. "I would be glad to be your navigator."

"What do you think, Dixon?" Cody asked, his voice was ringing with excitement.

"I think you two will have a real business someday, but I'm concerned about all those strangers crossing through the Ticonderoga. There goes my privacy." Dixon smiled as he answered.

"The Ticonderoga is so large," Cody said, "you may never see another hunter."

"Did any other aircraft land at the airport around spring last year that could fly to the Ticonderoga and back?" Dixon asked.

"No," Jerry replied. "Our runways are too short for airplanes capable of flying long distances to land on. Large aircraft flying out of Windsor, though, are equipped to fly to Fairbanks without refueling."

Cody was reading Dixon's thoughts. *How did a murderer travel into the Ticonderoga to kill Luke and then vanish?*

"I've read that Boeing is experimenting with a helicopter that can travel long distances, with *less* fuel, and land in a thousand-square-foot area," Jerry said. "The article indicated other countries were interested in purchasing these copters or *stealth cops*, as they are called, as soon as they were available. The cost was like eight million dollars. I guess that leaves me out," he laughed.

"Where are these built?" Dixon asked.

"In New Mexico. They've only built five of them," Jerry replied. "Two of them are being tested by the United States Air Force. These have the latest technology in computers and arsenal. The US Coast Guard is using two of them for search-and-rescue, and the CIA is testing one. The article didn't specify what their copter's equipped with."

When Dixon heard *CIA*, he could hardly contain his anticipation. "If a helicopter like that flew into the Ticonderoga, wouldn't you know?" Dixon asked the ATC expert.

"Not necessarily," Jerry replied. "Our radar system does not cover the entire Ticonderoga area. If it did, the stealth cop would probably be undetected with our radar equipment. We are supposed to be notified by every aircraft that enters the fringes of our quadrant."

"But, if they didn't want us to know, then any aircraft could enter without our knowledge. If they do enter in the quadrant's airport at Shaloh, they must provide their type of aircraft. Proper identification numbers and location of flight are required. If they fail to do this, they are breaking the rules and regulations set up by the IFFA. If they are identified and found guilty of this crime, they can be fined and imprisoned, and they would definitely lose their pilot's license."

Dixon was struggling to come back to earth from his racing thoughts. "Thank you, Jerry, for the information you've shared with Cody and me. It will be held in strict confidence. Cody is flying me into the Ticonderoga tomorrow. Hey, good luck with your copter! Maybe all three of us will fly in it someday."

As they got in the car, Dixon asked Cody, "How long have you known Jerry?"

"Oh, I've known Jerry since high school. He was the smart one in the class. He's an okay guy."

"Seems like it," agreed Dixon.

On the return to Cody's house, he and Cody did not talk. They were absorbing what Jerry had told them. Cody parked the old jeep in the carport. They could smell his wife's cooking as they entered the back door. Linda, although only in her thirties, cooked the old-fashioned way. She fried chicken and mashed potatoes and topped the meal off with homemade pie.

"That was a great meal, Linda," Dixon said. "But, Cody, how do you stay so thin?"

"Just hard work and clean living," he laughed.

Although he had old friends back in Dovel, Dixon really enjoyed these new friends. He and Chris had enjoyed hanging out with different couples, but Cody and Linda seemed special. "I want to pick up supplies this afternoon," Dixon said. "Will Dan be flying tomorrow?"

"No he's not," Cody replied. "I'd like for him to go with me, but he had other plans. Why do you ask?"

"Well, since he's not going, I can take more supplies, and I want to take as much as your plane can carry." Dixon smiled.

Chapter 20

Cody and Dixon loaded down the jeep with canned goods, sugar, cured hams, oil for lamps, and a new tent. A new .45-caliber Smith & Wesson pistol and ammo for both guns. "I'm going to have to make two or three trips from where you drop me off to my cabin," Dixon said as they were loading. "That will take five or six days,"

Cody thought a moment and said, "You know, Dixon, I just thought of a friend of mine—Ol' Mike—who might be able to help us out. Let's go see him. Mike is the owner of Hunters Heaven, Shaloh's wilderness supply store."

Ol' Mike was a favorite of everyone in Shaloh. His store carried everything from toothpicks to rubber rafts, rifles to beef jerky. It was a flourishing business. Hunters Heaven sure looked like it would live up to its name, Dixon thought as they drove into the parking lot.

After introductions, Cody asked, "Do you have some of those drop-off cartons left?"

"Yeah," Mike answered, chewing on his cigar. "You know I bought five or six of those cartons four years ago, but they didn't sell very quick." He laughed. "Too expensive I guess. But I think I have a couple in the back room—if you're interested, make me an offer."

"Come on," Cody said as he motioned for Dixon to follow him. "Let's take a look."

Entering Mike's back room was like walking into the past. He had antique furniture stacked on old cook stoves; canoes hung from the roof, and there were deer and bear heads on the walls. They stepped over and ducked under axes, shovels, and scythes. "Here they are," Cody said as he moved a couple of mantel clocks off the cartons.

"I've never dropped these from my plane, but from what I've been told, if dropped properly you can pack dishes in these and they won't be broken. But I wouldn't guarantee it," Cody was saying. "Still, if we use these, we can drop all your supplies near your cabin and save you a lot of time and work. You can just walk in with what you'll need for the trek."

"Let's do it," Dixon replied. Mike smiled as Dixon peeled out the cash for the cartons. "Now I've got room for more supplies!" he laughed. Cody and Dixon loaded the jeep and headed for the airport. They would load the plane tonight and prepare it for flight in the morning.

As Dixon lay in bed, he contemplated about telling Cody why he came to the Ticonderoga and about the maps. He liked Cody and Linda and felt he could trust them. It would be nice to be able to get some things off his chest; talk out the puzzles.

He could smell the bacon and eggs from his bedroom. Linda was baking biscuits and making gravy when Dixon went into the kitchen. "I thought I would send you off with a full stomach," Linda laughed.

Linda enjoyed eating as much as she did cooking. She was overweight but not obese. She had a pretty face and personality plus.

"I'll have Cody bring you to my cabin," Dixon said. "I'll cook *you* a meal!"

Cody was walking in and heard the conversation. "We'll take you up on that, Dixon!" he exclaimed.

They arrived at the airport just after sunrise. It was a hazy and quiet July morning. Cody checked off his list as he inspected his plane. "The wind is from the south," he said as he pulled the wheel stops. "It's only six mph." The instructions on the side of the drop-off crates advised pilots not to make a drop if the wind was fifteen mph or more. According to the weather charts, the wind velocity in the Ticonderoga was between eight to ten mph. "We should be okay."

At six thirty AM, they were in the air. Cody's ETA was eleven thirty AM. If the drop-off of cartons at the cabin and Dixon on the lake went smoothly, he should be back in Shaloh by five thirty PM.

Dixon decided not to talk to Cody about the maps. He knew he would see him next month. Maybe then?

The red-and-white piper glided effortlessly over forest and lakes below. The lake appeared small and a deep blue. The hardwood and underbrush were still green. *It is truly a beautiful area*, Dixon thought. He looked at his watch, it was eleven AM. Cody was writing in his log book. "How do you know the exact location of my cabin?" Dixon asked. "It all looks the same from up here."

"When Dan and I flew over you, we logged the coordinates of the terrain and altitude. With that information, I can locate the exact area we were in. We are about fifty miles from your cabin right now," Cody said looking in his book. "Why don't you begin unfastening the cartons. We'll make one pass to determine where to make the drop."

Unfastening the cartons permitted Dixon an excellent view of the Ticonderoga as Cody descended. Wildlife scattered and ran in all directions.

In what seemed like just a few minutes, Cody exclaimed, "Here we are!"

Dixon strained his eyes to see his cabin. "We just need a small clearing to drop-off," Cody was saying. "Where is the cabin?" Dixon shouted.

"Don't you remember—Daniel and I flew over twice and did not see your cabin. We would not have spotted you at all without that bright clothing you laid on the ground. Your cabin is hidden in those hardwoods." Dixon thought of the pine limbs he put on the roof to retain heat—that would also hide the cabin from the air.

"See that spot there?" Cody was shouting. Dixon nodded his head. "I'll make two passes; just pull those latches I showed you, when I say *pull*."

Cody banked his piper and continued his descent. Dixon thought the plane would be hitting the treetops. "Pull!" Cody yelled.

The first carton released and crashed through the trees, falling to the ground. Dixon watched the carton bounce up several feet and land on a flat side. *That was pretty neat,* Dixon thought as he looked at Cody and gave a thumbs up. The second carton was just as accommodating. Cody headed toward the lake. When they arrived, the water was calm and the piper landed without a bump.

Dixon and Cody agreed that on August twenty-first Cody would return, weather permitting. Dixon would start his trip to the lake on the eighteenth and be there when Cody arrived.

Chapter 21

Dixon was glad to be back on the Ticonderoga. He knew darkness would arrive soon and decided to stay by the lake on his first night back. He brought food to supply him for the two days' hike to his cabin. All he had to do was set up his tent and build a small fire for light and protection. As night quickly fell, he could hear the coyotes howling on the Ticonderoga. He checked his new .45 pistol, loaded his rifle, and closed up his tent. He crawled into his sleeping bag and went to sleep. When Dixon awoke, the sun was peeking over the eastern horizon. It was a warm morning, but the days seldom reached the eighties on the Ticonderoga.

He packed up and got an early start to his cabin. Since he'd packed so lightly, he wondered if he could make it to his cabin in one day. He hiked about two miles and remembered this was the area where he'd heard those voices last year and found Luke. It gave him an eerie feeling. He thought about checking Luke's grave, now that he knew who it was, but he decided against it. He wanted to get to his cabin by nightfall.

The sun set in the Ticonderoga woods, and Dixon was still two or three hours away from his cabin. He had purchased a helmet with a flashlight at Hunters Heaven and put it on, continuing his travel. It was still warm, even for late July. A full moon was beginning to appear in the east. He made it to his cabin in less than three hours. As he approached, he could see the two large cartons he and Cody had dropped. He examined the outside of the cartons and they appeared to have withstood the drop. *I'll unload these in the morning,* he thought as he walked to his cabin door.

Dixon had installed a strong latch on his door but not a lock. When he was going to leave his cabin for a few days, he would lay a short piece of fishing line on top of his door that would be visible on the outside if the door was opened. The fishing line would fall on the floor of the cabin.

Dixon flashed his light on the top of the door before entering. The fishing line wasn't there! Dixon pulled his .45 pistol from his holster. When he entered his cabin, he flashed his light in all directions. There was no one in the cabin. He lit several lamps and decided to start a fire in his stove, so he could make coffee.

As he proceeded to light the fire, he realized the handle to the stove top lid was lying on the stove. He always left the handle *in* the lid. The coffee can was always on the top shelf by the stove. Now it was on the second shelf. He started to look closer around the cabin.

It was soon evident that someone had been there. It appeared they had moved furniture, books, food, and dishes and possibly attempted to replace them as they were. He could tell by the dust on these items that it had been two or three weeks since they had been moved. Dixon was angry at the intrusion. There was little hunting in the summertime on the Ticonderoga, so he doubted that hunters were the culprits.

He fried some bacon he had brought with him. Finishing his meal and drinking his coffee, his mind was rewinding all that had occurred in the last few months. *There are people aware that I am in possession of certain papers: Ted, Tara, Mary Jo, maybe the FBI and the CIA, and who else, I don't know,* Dixon thought.

Chris' grandfather was in the Ticonderoga before his death. These papers—or maps as Dixon knew them—contained information that was secret, valuable, or both! He needed to sort out the information from these maps before anyone else did. He secured his cabin door on the inside and put his .45 by his pillow and fell asleep, happy to be in his own bed again.

The first morning after his return to his cabin, the sun was bright and the day was warm. He unpacked the cartons and was surprised how much food and supplies he'd purchased. He would have plenty, along with the meat he would hunt for. *I can still make one more cycle from where I stopped last fall exploring the Ticonderoga,* he thought.

Chapter 22

Back in Dovel, Tara had just explained Dixon's return to the Ticonderoga to Ted. He had become angry at Tara when she called to tell him that Dixon had left.

"You had plenty of time to call me!" he yelled on the phone. "Did you sleep with him last night?" he yelled again. "Did he tell you anything?"

"No!" Tara replied. "I tried to make love with him, but he pulled away. He wasn't going to tell me any more than he told you."

"I can find out his destination when he leaves Windsor," Ted barked. "I'll call the chief of police up there and tell him it's a family emergency."

"Ted, we've got to be careful," Tara replied. "If someone does locate him and he calls you, what are you going to say to him?"

"I'll tell the chief all we want to know is his location, and we will contact him. That is routine procedure unless I request assistance."

"Once we find out where he is . . . *if* we do . . . what's our next step?" Tara asked.

"We'll have to take things one step at a time," Ted replied. "He will be flying to another city."

"When we know that location, I'm hoping we can determine his destination from there."

"Oh, Ted," Tara exclaimed. "Are we getting too involved in this?" Sometimes, I wish we never—"

"Hold it!" Ted snapped. "We *are* involved. This is big, Tara, maybe more than we realize!"

Tara knew Ted was obsessed with the information he'd received from her and from the investigation into Chris' murder. Now Tara was having mixed emotions. After many meetings with Ted during his investigation of Chris' murder, they'd become involved. Ted was telling her he loved her, but she wasn't sure if it was love or a sexual response to the intense situation. When Ted filed for divorce from Mary Jo, Tara had been shocked. She did not approve and had threatened to break up their relationship.

Tara's advances toward Dixon were Ted's idea and calculated for one purpose: to pull information from him. Ted wanted to know exactly where Dixon was living. Although her attempt to seduce Dixon had failed, Tara's conscience had begun to bother her. His gentle rejection of her, his integrity touched her deeply, and before he left, Tara found she was actually falling in love with him. Now she and Ted were involved in something that could not have a good effect on her relationship with Dixon.

"This may be big," Tara was saying, "but is it so big that we are losing our senses? We don't know exactly what we are looking for, or even if Dixon *has* these papers. I think we should tell him everything that we know this far. He is our friend, you know—or have you forgotten that?"

"Tara, you don't understand! I don't believe Dixon knows the value of these papers. We know they contain information of *international* concern. We should know soon what that information is."

"You've said that for two years," Tara replied.

"That's how I know the information on these papers is important—"

Ted was speaking when all of a sudden Tara's telephone went dead for a fraction of a second. She interrupted Ted. "Did you notice that?" she asked.

"What?"

"My phone quit for a second."

"No, I didn't hear anything on this end," Ted replied. After a pause Ted said, "I'll be over tonight. I'll call Lacoff's and make reservations for dinner."

Tara wondered why he was so abrupt. "We will continue this discussion tonight," she thought. "I just want out."

Ted arrived early, and Tara was not ready. When she came out of her bedroom, she saw Ted replacing the cap on the speaker part of the telephone. "What are you doing?" she asked.

"Just fixing a drink," Ted replied while placing his index finger on his lips. "I made early reservations. Are you ready?"

Tara noticed that Ted had driven his personal car. He always drove the police car during the week, even when they went out together. He seemed apprehensive tonight as he opened her door.

"Has your phone ever done that before?"

"No, I don't think so."

"I believe your phone line has been tapped," he continued, "so we're not going to Lacoff's for dinner."

"Who would tap my phone and why?" Tara exclaimed with a concerned frown on her forehead.

"About two weeks before Dixon showed up," Ted began, "I received a call from Scott Higgins. He is a special agent of the FBI. He questioned me about my investigation of Chris' murder. Before I answered him, I questioned the FBI's participation in a murder in my jurisdiction. He said his office had reason to believe this murder was orchestrated by an *underground faction*. Mr. Higgins and I met when Dixon was here. He asked me if I knew of Dixon's whereabouts, and I told him he was staying with you a few weeks. I couldn't lie to him. If he found out, I would be under suspicion."

"Why didn't you tell me all this?" Tara demanded. "Why didn't you tell Dixon?"

"I didn't tell him because I still don't know his level of participation in all this. And I remembered your reaction when the FBI was mentioned before, so I didn't want you to be freaking out about my talking to them while Dixon was still here."

"What else are you not telling me?" she wanted to know. "I want to know everything! If someone is listening to every phone call I make, what else are they monitoring?"

"I don't know the answer to that," Ted said, "but if your phone is tapped and if they are monitoring your moves, they know I come to your house often. That is why *I* haven't been informed of their activities. For what it's worth, I don't think any of this began until I told Higgins that Dixon was staying with you. At this point, their main interest is in Dixon. Higgins thought Dixon would stay longer. Your phone is tapped to listen to his conversations. The conversation you and I had today on the phone was . . . not private. The things we discussed will be questionable at the least. We talked of Dixon's destination and how I would get it through Windsor's chief. We talked about the papers, how important they are, and we even mentioned *international concern.*"

Tara was terrified! "Do you think they will be coming to pick us up for questioning?"

Ted pulled into the Mist. It was a small, quaint restaurant with booths that were dark and private. "We can talk inside," Ted said.

They ordered their drinks, and Ted thumped his fingers on the table. Tara never saw him this nervous before.

"The FBI doesn't know that we know your telephone is tapped," Ted said. "You must continue to use your phone as usual. Make your regular calls, including the ones to me, and I will call you as usual. Since we are aware of being listened to, we will adjust our conversations. We can't just drop our discussion of Dixon abruptly. We will continue to mention our concerns over his location and how we would like to visit him. We'll also discuss his health and his injured arm. The FBI aren't dummies; I don't know how long it will take them to realize we know we're being listened to. Although they will dissect the conversation you and I had today, there is no evidence of wrongdoing. Just be aware that, since your phone is tapped, you are probably also under surveillance. I'm sure they saw me pick you up tonight, but we weren't followed here. They probably went to Lacoff's to wait for us." He faintly smiled.

"Ted, I don't like this at all! I think we should just drop it. Telephone conversations taped, our homes are under surveillance—it's time to quit!"

"We can't just drop it," Ted insisted. "At least I can't. The murder is still under investigation, and now the FBI is involved. I have a meeting with this Mr. Higgins on Friday at two o'clock. I'm sure by then he will know Dixon has left. If he informs me of the telephone tap and his knowledge of our conversation, you and I will probably be interrogated. We must be sure we are saying the same thing. If he does *not* tell me, that will indicate they are hoping to receive more information from us through Dixon's calls and surveillance of us. So, until he and I talk, just do the things you normally do. Meet me here Friday night, say eight PM. I'll make sure I'm not followed."

Tara picked at her Caesar salad while Ted started on his prime rib. By now their appetites were gone. Returning to Tara's house, she could not hide her anxiety. Her eyes wide open, she looked at any car that remained behind them over two minutes. Arriving home, Ted drove completely around Tara's block. They saw no one suspicious, but Ted decided not to go inside. They waved at each other as he drove away.

Chapter 23

M r. Higgins arrived at Ted's office at two PM precisely. He was accompanied by two other men. Ted swallowed hard when the three entered his office. It was a hot July day, but all three men wore dark business suits and ties.

"Mr. Hands," Scott Higgins began, "this is Dwight Cox, special agent with the department. Mr. Cox operates out of our Pentagon offices. And this is Wendall Hartzel. Mr. Hartzel is chief deputy director of the Central Intelligence Agency, also headquartered at Langley, VA". Ted shook hands and asked the gentlemen to be seated. He was trying to conceal his nervousness. "Would you like some coffee or soda?" he asked.

"No," Higgins answered as he looked out the office door and closed it. "Please tell your secretary to hold your calls until we are done here." Ted complied. "Mr. Hands," Higgins began, "we know you have been involved in the investigation of Chris O'Laverty's murder from day one. We are aware of your acquaintance with her and her husband prior to the murder. How well did you know Mr. O'Laverty?"

Ted was turning noticeably pale. He realized this group of men knew much more than they were letting on. He knew he must be truthful. "I've known Dixon O'Laverty for years," Ted replied. "We went hunting and fishing together. We ate out occasionally along with our wives, but we were never *close* friends. Just good friends." He smiled.

Higgins continued, "The list you gave me of the contents of his safe involved cash, some jewelry, and papers. Do you have a list of the papers?"

"Yes," Ted replied, pulling files from his desk. "This is the list of papers Dixon—Mr. O'Laverty—gave me: marriage license, mortgage papers, wills, titles to the cars, and life insurance policies."

"Would Mr. O'Laverty have any reason to withhold information regarding other papers that might have been in the safe?" Higgins asked.

"Not that I'm aware of ... unless it was something ... you know, *personal* ... that he felt wasn't important enough to mention."

"Mr. Hands," Agent Hartzel cut in, "approximately six months into your investigation of Mrs. O'Laverty's murder, you sought the names of several released convicts whose MO's were similar to her murderer ..."

"Correct," Ted replied.

"According to your records you interviewed one ex-con who was out on bail on other charges."

"That's right," Ted replied. "I had that interview about a year after the murder."

"Your record is rather vague, Mr. Hands. It stated this ex-con had a rock-solid alibi for his whereabouts on the day of Mrs. O'Laverty's murder. It continues . . . you verified his alibi and found it to be completely valid and true. Nonetheless. the report does not contain the facts—the location of said whereabouts, a validating witness name, or the verifying evidence of his alibi. Is there a reason for this incompleteness?"

"The report was complete to my satisfaction," Ted replied. "This ex-con was in the Wells General Hospital in Birmingham, Virginia, recovering from appendicitis surgery on the day of the murder. I did not include this information in my report. If an alibi is found to be valid and true, I usually do not include all pertinent information unless required in court proceedings."

"This ex-con—I believe his name is Leo, is that correct?"

"Yes," Ted Replied

"Did Leo give you any information concerning the investigation of Mrs. O'Laverty's murder?"

Beads of sweat formed on Ted's forehead. He knew this CIA agent must have information about a discussion Leo and Ted had during his investigation. "Leo told me of his cellmate in prison," Ted began. "The cellmate's name was Harry Barnes. Harry was in prison for killing a man in Washington, DC. The murder was designed as a hit-and-run accident. Harry did not know his assigned victim was a powerful figure in the political arena. Before his arrest, he was told there was another job *they* wanted done. (Harry never met any of his employers—or clients, whatever you want to call them. Negotiations were completed by third-party contacts who picked up and delivered papers and money.) Harry understood he was to make arrangements to go to Dovel, Maryland. He was told there were important papers his *clients* wanted. Instructions would follow after his arrival. He would be paid a half million dollars for those papers. He was angry, he told Leo, because he never got the papers, and on his return to DC, he was arrested for the hit-and-run. A week after Harry shared this story with Leo, Harry was stabbed to death in the prison yard. Rumor had it—*prison* rumor—that he was killed because of CIA investigations into a homicide in Dovel. Leo was afraid the same thing was gonna happen to him."

Hartzel's face was reddening. "Did you share this discussion with anyone else?" he asked.

"No," Ted answered. "I thought it was far-fetched."

"This is obstruction of justice, Hands!" he exclaimed. "You withheld important information. The CIA should have been contacted after hearing an accusation like this!"

"I did not . . . contact *any* other agency . . . for several reasons!" Ted protested, doing his best to stay cool and not stammer through this. "This story was coming from an ex-con who was out on bail. I didn't know how much of it was the truth . . . or if any of it was. Blaming the cops is a pretty bad habit with these guys; blaming the CIA is what the crazier ones do. I figured that's all it was. There were other homicides in Dovel during that six-month period as well. If the CIA had an interest in a homicide in Dovel, I was unaware of it!" He took a sip from a half liter of bottled water sitting on his desk. It was three days old, but he didn't care.

"I did contact officials at the federal penitentiary, and they told me Harry had died of a heart attack. 'So that's it,' I thought. I asked a couple more questions about Harry's case and was referred to the prosecuting attorney in DC. I was doing my due diligence. This guy, the prosecutor, he told me Harry's arrest and conviction were nothing unusual. I realized I was receiving answers to pacify me. If anybody was obstructing, it was on your end. And believe me, I wondered.

"It took me three months to acquire the name of the hit-and-run *victim!* At that time, I also got a list of his heirs . . . that's when I found out Chris O'Laverty was his granddaughter! Now I had a hunch that Harry came down to Dovel to steal papers from Chris and, in the process, tortured and murdered her. Was he telling the truth to Leo that he didn't get them, or did he like what he saw and was trying to throw his clients off? The question remains, where are those papers that were worth killing for and who wanted them? I am still in the process of try to finalize this case. Chris O'Laverty was not just a citizen of Dovel, Mr. Higgins—and I'm responsible for protecting and serving all of them. But she was a friend of my wife's and the wife of a friend."

"Mr. Hands . . ." It was Dwight Cox's turn to talk. "You said you did not share the information Leo told you to anyone. Have you discussed these . . . papers of unknown value with anyone?"

Ted hesitated. He had interrogated suspects and knew Cox was ready to pounce on him if his answer was not consistent with what they already knew. "Yes, I have," Ted replied. With another friend, a neighbor of the O'Laverty's.

"Are you and this lady intimately involved?"

"We have been for about two years," Ted again replied.

"What was the purpose of sharing this information?"

Ted stood up and walked over to the window. He didn't want to look them in the eyes. "By now," he started, "you gentlemen know that I know that Tara's telephone is tapped. I also know the conversation Tara and I had on Wednesday has been taped and you probably have it with you." The three gentlemen looked at each other but did not otherwise move. "You know that I am attempting to locate where Dixon is living. When I said to Tara, I don't believe Dixon knows the value of these papers, I realized that I don't know this value either. I don't even know what the papers consist of." Ted turned around and sat back down at his desk and looked at each man in the eyes. "I do know," he said, "that three people have been murdered . . . that I'm aware of . . . because of these papers. That gives them value to me.

"My professional duty was to notify Dixon of my findings. That's where I have failed. At this point, I do not know for sure if Dixon has the papers. I presume he does—though who knows, maybe Harry got them and squirreled them away somewhere, to be discovered some other day. I did not contact the FBI or the CIA, because of other reasons, too." Ted held his head down. "I know Harry Barnes murdered Chris, but what evidence do I have? So I've kept the case open. And I didn't tell Dixon anything that I learned from the investigation, because . . . well . . . I thought if I could get my hands on those papers, I would benefit politically and financially."

He looked away, knowing his career in law enforcement was over. "Tara has done nothing wrong or illegal," he continued. "Her involvement in attempting to locate the papers was directed by me. She thought I was trying to avenge Chris' murder. I'm truly sorry."

Chapter 24

"Ted," Mr. Higgins spoke more personably now, "in the last two weeks we have thoroughly searched your background. We found you have been involved in law enforcement for fifteen years and your reputation has been impeccable.

"In 1992, you were cleared for access to top-secret documents in a case involving a mobster from Baltimore versus the State of Maryland. The mobster was indicted because of your intense investigation. But your handling of the case of Mrs. O'Laverty could be construed as an obstruction of justice by the federal government. There is a possibility of fines and imprisonment."

Ted nodded. "I understand, but I will fight that charge. The only thing I have obstructed, and I'm not saying it's not every bit as bad, is the widower's right to know."

Higgins asked Ted to step outside the door. Ted imagined the worst scenario: *I could be arrested and jailed immediately.* He thought of the horror stories he'd heard of former law enforcement sent to jail—and how they were mistreated and even killed by retaliatory convicts. *What about Tara? They will be interrogating her next. If she tells the truth as I did—*

His thoughts were interrupted when Higgins called him back into the office.

"Mr. Hartzel, Mr. Cox, and myself cannot make deals, but we do make recommendations. We just spoke with Assistant Director Humphrey from the FBI. He is very involved in the recovery of these papers. We have been directed to inform you of their contents and the potentially catastrophic results to parts of the world if they get into the wrong hands. That's why it is crucial these papers—actually, they are *maps*—are found by our government.

"You know Dixon personally, and we know he considers you a friend. This knowledge and friendship will enable us to approach Dixon . . . when we locate him. We believe that Dixon does not know the value of these maps, as we will now call them, but that he is actively engaged in trying to find out.

"It appears that he has not broken any law in his pursuit of finding the reason for the maps, but he has not been transparent about them either. If you will assist us in locating Dixon—hopefully before he finds the definite location of the . . . item . . . on the map, you will be absolved of any charges. We also have determined your friend Miss Copley has not broken any law. But we do want to meet with her as soon as possible—tonight if possible. We will not give either of you any top-secret information on this case, and she must be informed not to divulge or discuss this with any person. Maintaining secrecy is federal law. If either of you breaks that law, you will be subject to immediate arrest. She will be notified that we will continue to tape her telephone conversations—in case Dixon or any other party in the case contacts her—and will keep her under surveillance. This is being done for her protection."

"I will call her now," Ted replied, "and I will assist you in locating Dixon."

He picked up the phone and called Tara.

"Per Mr. Humphrey's direction, we are to make you aware of all aspects of this case."

Mr. Higgins opened his briefcase. It was clear that he had accepted Mr. Humphrey's direction, and that any ill feelings toward Ted were gone.

"Mrs. O'Laverty's grandfather was Frank Norris," Hartzel began. "His office was in the Pentagon where he was employed by the US government. He also received assignments from the CIA due to his influence, intelligence, and his ability to speak several languages. On one of his assignments, he was approached by a Libyan National who was pro-American. This Libyan had information for the location of supergrade plutonium. One missile of supergrade plutonium used in a W80 warhead could destroy the city of Baltimore.

"Mr. Norris, knowing the destructive potential of this mixture and its ramifications, agreed to pay the Libyan for this information. Arrangements were made, and the CIA deposited five million dollars into an account in Switzerland under a Libyan assigned code number at the time when Frank received the information from the Libyan. This all occurred in the American Embassy near Libya. From this information, Frank was able to make contact with informants in Libya who were sympathetic with US policy. With this assistance from the Libyan National underground and the informants, the plutonium was delivered to Frank Norris. The next day, as Frank was preparing to fly to the USA via CIA special jet, he received a call from his asset. All of the Libyan Nationals involved in the finding and stealing of the plutonium had been assassinated, along with their families. He was calling from Switzerland and was fearful for his own life. He told Frank Libyan radicals would soon find out where the plutonium was delivered. They had their *ways* of extracting information.

Frank Norris was not aquainted with the two pilots who had been assigned by the CIA to fly him out of Lybia. He was informed they were not privileged to know what material they were carrying on the plane. Not known to Frank was that the CIA pilots originally ordered to fly the airplane, had been murdered and replaced by Lybian pilots. The jet flew out of the Libyan International Airport, destination Alaska. An hour into the flight, Frank realized the aircraft was banking slowly. Since they were flying over water, he knew the plane was turning around.

"He opened the cockpit door and was facing a .45-caliber revolver held by one of the pilots. He looked at the other pilot and could see the nylon cord around his neck. His eyes were open, and Frank knew he was dead. He also knew the pilot with the pistol was probably a defector. The defector told Frank to get back in his seat; they were flying back to Libya. According to Frank's report, this defector didn't know Frank was an experienced pilot. Going back into the cockpit, the pilot turned his back on Frank. Frank jumped him, and in the ensuing fight, the pilot's neck was broken. Frank turned the aircraft around again, back toward Alaska."

Chapter 25

Wendall Hartzel continued with the story of Frank Norris and the suitcase of plutonium. "When he arrived in Alaska, records indicate Frank asked for a helicopter equipped with extra fuel tanks. He knew the jet would be held up a few days for the authorities to remove the bodies and comb the airplane and issue a release. With Frank's position and influence, they did not question his request. The plutonium was transferred to the helicopter.

"Airport authorities in Alaska reminded Frank he would have to refuel in Accordia. This is where the mystery deepens. Frank never landed in Accordia. Where he did land and refuel is unknown. We do know the FFA received correspondence from the IFFA concerning irregularities in Frank's flight plan. At that time, the assistant to the director of the FFA and Frank were close friends. Between them, they were able to put an end to any investigation of his flight from Alaska, including where he refueled prior to landing in DC." Hartzel put down his paperwork. "Let's take a break and have a cold drink. I'll let Dwight finish the bizarre episode."

Ted got up and left the room to go to the restroom. Walking down the hall, he met Tara. She was nervous, and Ted could see in her eyes she had been crying. "Are they still here?" she asked. "Yes, and they want to talk to you," Ted stated, "and all you—"

Tara interrupted. "What's going to happen to us? What should I say?" She began crying again.

"Listen to me," Ted said, "just tell them the absolute truth. Then listen to what they have to say. Turns out we're all on the same side. And it's Dixon's side too. Follow their instructions and what their plans are concerning you. Believe me, Tara, this is going to be okay. I can't say any more except we must work with them." Ted took Tara by the arm and led her into his office.

After introductions, Ted told the three gentlemen what he said to Tara in the hallway. He excused himself and told them he would be waiting in the next office whenever they were ready for him to return.

An hour later, Tara came to him. She hugged him and cried. "I'm so relieved!" she exclaimed. "I don't understand all of what's going on, but they have my cooperation."

Ted stroked her hair and kissed her forehead, nodding his approval and shared relief. "I have to go back in."

Dwight Cox was an imposing gentleman, tall with broad shoulders and a square jaw. He spoke with authority and knowledge. "When Frank landed in DC in the helicopter, my agents and Wendall's here were there to meet him and pick up the plutonium. It wasn't in the helicopter.

"I was immediately notified and made arrangements to meet Norris. I called Mr. Humphrey, who would join me in debriefing our operative.

"I'd known Frank Norris for many years," Cox continued, "but when he arrived at my office, I knew he was deeply troubled. He wouldn't look me in the eyes, and he did not smile. He looked completely exhausted from his long trip. The secretary and Mr. Humphrey arrived soon after Frank. They had been researching Frank's background and employment history with the government. I am going to read to you the complete transcripts of our conversation that took place in that meeting: 'Frank,' that's the secretary of defense talking . . .

"We have a serious problem here and you are aware of what that problem is? We are confident that you have a valid explanation of where the plutonium is, why it was not in the copter when you arrived.'"

"I can tell you why the plutonium was not in the copter, but I will not tell you—nor anyone—where it is," Frank replied.

"Mr. Norris," Mr. Humphrey began, "you know the potential destruction of plutonium as well as we do. The moment we realized it was not in the helicopter, a flag was raised as to your credibility. When you tell us why it was not onboard, you must tell us where it is. Your credibility and reputation are not only at stake, but without full cooperation—and if you withhold information detrimental to the safety and defense of the US government—you can be arrested. Am I clear on this?"

"Yes, sir," Frank began, "allow me to be clear on my reasons to answer you as I did. The Libyan radicals will go to any means to retrieve this plutonium. They will kill anyone who interferes with their mission. In my report to Wendall Hartzel, you will find their involvement in the murder of the Libyan Nationals, our CIA assets and their families. The defector killed the pilot of that jet, and I still don't know why he didn't kill me immediately? After I was forced to kill him, I searched his briefcase. He had orders to return me to them, *dead or alive*."

"There was a substantial deposit in a Swiss account in his name. That amount would be doubled when he delivered me and the plutonium to their headquarters. The letter continued, 'Should your mission fail, not only will Frank Norris and any of his family members be killed, but you and any of your family will be executed.' The only family member I have left is my granddaughter, Mr. Humphrey. I love her more than anyone. I don't want to jeopardize her life because of my involvement concerning this situation. The defector failed in his mission. My granddaughter and I are now on their list. I decided that if I put the plutonium in a safe hiding place where it would never be found, our lives might be spared. The radicals will know it never reached the United States. If they contact or kidnap me, I will tell them that I destroyed the plutonium. If they believe that, I might be murdered anyway because of disbelief or anger at me. Thinking the plutonium is destroyed, though, my granddaughter would be spared. Killing her would serve them no purpose.

"I'm getting older, Mr. Humphrey," Frank continued, "and my position requires a younger, more energetic person. I will be submitting my resignation. I did not bring the plutonium to the United States, but I cannot and will not tell you or anyone where it is. The cycle would begin all over again and innocent lives would be lost. We don't want that on our conscience."

"Frank retired one month later," said Dwight Cox, continuing, "and one month after retirement, he was killed by the hit-and-run driver, Harry Barnes."

"Around two months after his death," Hartzel said, "his replacement, a Mr. Cordell, was receiving a new desk. The delivery man removed all the drawers to reduce the weight of the desk. Mr. Cordell noticed an envelope taped to the underneath side of one of the drawers. It was addressed to the secretary of defense. Mr. Cordell delivered it to my office, whereupon I carried it to the secretary's office. He opened it immediately and shared the contents with me.

"After reading the letter, we believe that Frank did not anticipate its discovery so soon, if ever. He referred to the plutonium case that occurred a few months prior to the date of the letter concerning him and the US government:

I informed the secretary of defense at that time and the assistant secretary and an FBI agent that I have destroyed the plutonium. This was not true. I put it in a safe hiding place. The reason for my actions was to protect my family and the United States government. I made maps of where the plutonium is hidden. If I am alive when this letter is read, contact me, and I will turn the maps over to your office. If I have passed away, the location will never be known.

Frank signed the letter, "Forgive Me."

"Ted," Hartzel continued now, "we did not have a reason to go through Frank's apartment immediately after his death. This letter was found two months later. His granddaughter had already sold or given away his furniture and other items.

"We concluded at that time that the maps were disposed of without knowledge of their content. Now we believe the maps were found during this period of time and kept by the granddaughter. We are sure those are the papers that Dixon has in his possession. Somehow, the Libyan radicals suspected Chris had these maps and that is where Harry Barnes entered the picture. He blew it and was killed because of his failure to obtain the maps. Now we must find Dixon, the maps, and the plutonium before the Libyans do," Hartzel said.

Chapter 26

Dixon packed his supplies and started out on his two-week search. After one week out, he was beginning his turnaround. Although enjoying his exploration, he was again not finding anything that resembled the indications on his map. He arrived at his cabin a week later without any success. Cooking his meal, he thought about Cody and Linda. Cody would be back in one week to pick him up. *I'm going to tell Cody about the maps,* Dixon thought. *If Jerry and I could fly over the Ticonderoga in the copter and locate the indicators on the map . . . I think I'll do it,* he concluded.

There was a chill in the air the morning of August eighteenth. Dixon began his journey to the lake to meet Cody. It was the beginning of fall in the Ticonderoga. Dixon arrived at the lake the next evening. Cody would be arriving before noon the next day, and Dixon was anxious to see him.

He was surprised to see the red-and-white piper before he could hear the engine. Cody landed effortlessly. Cody waved and helped Dixon board the plane. The trip to Shaloh Airport went fast. Cody and Dixon chatted about everything, but nothing important. When they arrived, Jerry was just going off-duty.

"How's that copter coming?" Dixon asked.

"Pretty good," Jerry replied. "Now that we've got most of the parts we needed."

"Are you going to have it ready next spring?" Dixon chuckled as he asked.

"Probably not until summer; the old barn isn't heated. That limits the number of days left that I can work on it this fall," Jerry answered. "I checked out the cost of enclosing part of the inside of the barn so I could install a heating unit, but that costs a lot of money. I'll just have to work as late as I can this fall and close it up until spring."

Dixon was disappointed to hear this. He wanted to start searching the Ticonderoga by helicopter as soon as spring arrived. He didn't mention any of this to Jerry, however.

Jerry continued, "I'd like to talk to you and Cody tomorrow . . . things have happened since you left. I'm late now for an appointment, so call me in the morning."

"Okay," Dixon answered.

When they arrived at Cody's house, Linda was cooking up a storm. By the time they completed their meal and cleaned up the mess, it was after eight PM. Dixon decided to wait until the next day to call Tara and Mary Jo. In Dovel, it would be after ten PM eastern time.

Jerry called at seven thirty the next morning. "I don't need to go in until noon today," he was saying to Cody. "Could you and Dixon come to the house?"

"Sure," Cody replied. "We'll be there around nine."

When they arrived, Jerry was pouring three cups of coffee. They went into his office, where he pulled out a log book. "This log records all of your flights in and out of Shaloh Airport for the month of July," he said to Cody. "The reason I brought it home is because I might want to rewrite it. If I do, you and I will have to agree on its contents or modify a log after its been entered."

Cody was puzzled. "Why would you want to rewrite the log?" he asked.

"I was beginning to enter July's flight logs into the IFFA system. Before I got to yours, I received a phone call from a Dwight Cox out of Baltimore. He identified himself as a special agent for the FBI out of DC. He was calling from the Baltimore International Airport. The senior traffic controller came on the line, introduced himself, and asked that I cooperate with Mr. Cox. Cox came back on the phone and requested a copy of the logs of flights that arrived from Baltimore via the Windsor Airport during the last two weeks of July. He was especially interested in the passenger list. I told Mr. Cox I could fax him a copy as soon as I completed my transmission into the IFFA system."

"Do you get requests like this very often?" Dixon asked.

"No," Jerry answered. "I've never had a request from the States like this. I told Mr. Cox I would require a signed letter from the IFFA allowing me to release this information. Cox said he would contact the FFA and they would expedite the requests to IFFA to authorize this release. I received authorization yesterday. Now, my question is to you two: is there a reason I should rewrite the log or send it as-is?"

Cody looked at Dixon with a puzzled expression. "I don't know of any reason to alter the log, do you?"

"No, not with the flight from Windsor. But do they need to know of our flights into the Ticonderoga?" he asked Jerry.

"The only request I have now are the flights from Windsor via Baltimore to Shaloh," Jerry replied. "We are required by law to log every flight in and out of this airport, and that includes Cody's flight to the Ticonderoga. There were only two landings in Shaloh Airport from Windsor that originated in Baltimore in the last two weeks of July. You and Cody were one and the other one was a small UPS delivery and pickup flight. I can record that in a separate log. I would still be in the legal guidelines, but if the IFFA requested them, I would have to submit those also."

Cody knew Dixon enjoyed his privacy. "What do you think?" He looked at Dixon.

"I don't want Jerry entering false information into the logs for my benefit," Dixon replied. "It sounds like they are looking for me, doesn't it?"

"Do you know why the FBI would be looking for you?" Cody asked.

Dixon looked at the two gentlemen and thought about all they had done for him. They had learned to trust each other. He thought about Cody and Linda's generosity and hospitality. They had all become close friends. "Let me start from the beginning," Dixon said.

He talked about his marriage to Chris and then of her tragic murder. He told them of the maps they found and of their plans to visit the Ticonderoga together someday. He discussed his attempt to locate the destination on the maps. He discussed his inability to locate any point of direction as indicated on them. He told them of the conversation between Mary Jo and the mention of the FBI and CIA, from Ted Hands and Tara. "That was the only time I heard FBI involvement until now, and that was secondhand hearsay. I wasn't sure I even believed it. But if the FBI is checking these flights to find where I am, then these maps must be of importance to the United States government."

"At this point," Jerry stated, "your name has not been mentioned. All they have requested is a list of names of passengers. When I send this copy of the logs today, you are actually the only passenger. Cody will be listed as the pilot, and UPS consisted of a pilot, copilot, and a navigator. If they are seeking you, Cody will be the next one they will want to contact."

"Cody," Dixon began, "if the FBI contacts you, be truthful with them. The only concern I have is anyone else knowing my exact location."

"I can show them where I met you on the lake," Cody said, "and your cabin is well hidden. I wouldn't have to tell them I know where it is."

"I will cooperate with the proper authorities," Dixon said. "If I was living in the United States, I would contact the FBI immediately. But since we are not in the United States, the FBI does not have any jurisdiction in Canada. They will have to go through the proper channels. Until I am contacted, I want to continue my own search. Cody, do not jeopardize your future. If you are asked for my exact location, you must cooperate."

"I don't know how long it would take to go through the proper channels," Cody began, "but I do know after I return from taking you back, the lake will begin to freeze within two or three weeks.

That would prevent me from returning to the Ticonderoga until spring."

"I am going to send the logs as requested," Jerry said, "only because the senior traffic controller in Windsor and I are acquainted with each other. It was his request that I cooperate with Mr. Cox."

Chapter 27

"Before I release any more confidential information to authorities in the US, I will request proper authorization as required through the French Internal Affairs or DFA. They will contact the IFFA, who will in turn again direct me. I would estimate it will take six to eight weeks to complete. Let's just play it by ear." Dixon was talking. "I will be going back tomorrow. If they want to talk to me, they'll have to wait until spring too, and that brings up another question I have. If I paid for enclosing part of your barn and installing a heating unit, would your copter be ready by spring?"

"Oh yeah," Jerry replied. "I would probably have it ready before spring, but I don't want you to spend your money for that."

"Well, it would be for me too," Dixon replied. "I would like for you and Cody to pick me up as soon as the weather permits next spring. We could fly over the Ticonderoga and maybe look for the indicators on the maps. What do you say?"

Cody spoke up. "I could help you, Jerry, and I'd be glad to fly with you to the Ticonderoga."

"Okay. I'll get someone started on the barn right away!" Jerry replied.

Dixon had told Mary Jo and Tara that he would call them. He was now apprehensive about talking to them. He didn't know who he could trust or who could put his life in danger, even inadvertently. *What do they know, and how do they know?* he wondered. *Will they tell me the truth?* The questions lingered as he dialed Tara's number.

"I told you I would be waiting!" she exclaimed, excited. "I miss you! How's the arm coming?" she asked.

"It's healing fine," Dixon replied, "and what have you been up to?"

Tara's voice tightened up as she answered. "Well, your house sold; the renters bought it," she said.

"That's great," Dixon replied, but noticing the change in her voice. "Anything else exciting in Dovel?" he chuckled. Tara hesitated. Although the FBI informed her that her telephone was no longer being tapped, she wasn't sure.

"Not really," she answered. "Are you going to call Ted? He was disappointed you left without saying good-bye. I told him you said you would call him."

"I'll call him next," Dixon replied. Tara and Dixon reminisced the times together over the summer. Dixon could hear the tension in Tara's voice. Tara asked Dixon to call her again as soon as he could.

He decided to call Mary Jo next. She was so glad to hear from him. Dixon asked if she heard any more about or from Ted and Tara?

"No, I haven't seen them or talked to either one since you left. Have you heard anything new?" she asked.

"I've heard some things, but can't give you any details until I know more. Until then, keep your chin up. I won't be calling you back until next spring."

"Will you be coming back then?" Mary Jo wanted to know.

"I might be, but it would be May. I'll let you know if I'm coming."

I didn't learn anything new from those two, Dixon thought as he hung up the phone. Someone had to tell the FBI of my flight plan from Baltimore to Windsor. He decided not to call Ted Hands just yet.

Frost was on the ground the next morning. "It's going to be an early winter," Cody was saying as he inspected his Piper. "That lake will be frozen by the end of September. Too bad the copter isn't done; Linda and I would fly in for Christmas," he chuckled.

"As soon as it is done," Dixon replied, "bring it in. I hope we have an early spring and you guys get it ready."

"We're planning on completion by the end of March," Cody said. "We'll be there!"

Flying out of Shaloh Airport, Dixon pondered Jerry's information, Tara's apprehension, and his beloved Chris. "All the times that Chris and I got those maps out, we studied, laughed, and dreamed. Now the FBI is involved, and who knows what lies ahead."

The flight to the Ticonderoga was the most beautiful Dixon had ever seen. The leaves were turning and the lake looked almost black. He was anxious to return to his cabin but realized that others knew of its location.

He had told Cody of the intrusion into his cabin when he came back in July. Now he wondered what he might find on his return. After they docked the Piper and unloaded the few supplies Dixon picked up, Cody asked Dixon if he wanted him to go to the cabin with him.

"I appreciate your offer, Cody; I'll be on guard," Dixon said. "It would take you at least three full days of traveling to the cabin and back and I would want you to spend a couple of days with me. Once this lake starts freezing, it doesn't take long to freeze over. I've got my .45 right here," he said and pulled back his jacket.

"Just be careful," Cody replied. "I haven't figured out where an intruder would come from and how they got here."

"You and Jerry get that copter together! I'll be there when you land," Dixon said. He watched as the Piper disappeared into the sky. For the first time since his arrival on the Ticonderoga almost three years ago, he felt alone and vulnerable.

He picked up his pack and headed for the cabin. When he arrived there, the door had not been disturbed. Everything was as he had left it. The next month, he hunted, fished, and picked berries. Although he had plenty of supplies, he wanted to be prepared. Snow began falling in late September. He finished his coffee, put away the maps, and filled his old stove with wood. As he lay in bed, he reflected back on the past summer.

Cody, Linda, and Jerry had become close friends. His old friends back in Dovel had changed. He was now beginning his third winter and was more determined than ever to solve the mystery of the maps. The falling snow had slowed down by morning. There was an accumulation of several inches. He made his coffee a little stronger. He was going to be outside most of the day. He had purchased snowshoes back at Hunters Heaven and was anxious to try them out. He would do small-game hunting at the same time.

Chapter 28

The trees were heavy with snow. He had been hunting two hours when he heard a strange sound. Whatever it was, it sounded far away. He cocked his rifle and headed in the direction of the sound. And then it quit after about five minutes. He kept walking in that direction. In about ten minutes, the noise started again, and then again began to fade away. He could not determine what it was. Although he could no longer hear any sound, he continued in the same direction for twenty minutes.

Up ahead the evergreens were more visible. As he got closer, he could see the snow on the ground and trees was scattered and appeared to have been blown away. Then he noticed five imprints in the snow with rudders He knew immediately what he'd found. A helicopter had landed and left. He walked to the edge of the opening and could see several footprints. He pulled his .45 from his jacket. It appeared that four people had made the prints. It began to snow again.

The two sets of prints indicated the persons had put on snowshoes and headed out into the Ticonderoga. *The other two must have flown out in the copter,* he thought. Dixon's heart rate increased. He could feel his hands sweating in his gloves. He attempted to follow the footprints, but they soon became covered with new snow. He started back to his cabin with his .45 in hand. *Hunters don't travel in helicopters!* he thought as he was walking. *If it was someone Jerry or Cody sent, they could have landed closer to the cabin. Could the FBI and CIA send someone to find me?* he wondered.

When he arrived in his cabin's proximity, the snow had stopped falling. He circled the area and looked for snow prints or other signs that might indicate someone had been there. He did not find anything. The fishing line on his cabin door was intact. Still, he entered cautiously. When he found that no one was in the cabin or the area, he breathed a sigh of relief.

By now, it was late afternoon. He would fix some supper and attempt to rest. He wouldn't sleep. He knew there were two people out in the Ticonderoga. *Were they prepared to spend the night in the dark cold terrain?* he wondered. *Were they looking for him? Were they friends or foes?*

If the snow did not fall again, he would search the area again tomorrow.

When morning arrived, he decided to walk around the cabin area before preparing breakfast. He strapped on his .45. He could still see his footprints in the snow from last night. There was no evidence that anyone else had been in the area. He knew as he fired up his stove heavier to cook breakfast that the smoke would be visible to anyone within a mile of the cabin. *I've got to eat,* he thought, *and I've got to continue to live as though I'm unaware of other people in the area.* If these were the same ones who disturbed his cabin before, they knew where the cabin was.

He finished his breakfast and, as he was packing food for his day on the Ticonderoga, someone was knocking on his door! He took his .45 out of the holster and held the gun behind him. When he opened the door, he was facing a large man with a rifle over his shoulder.

"Hello, sir," the huge hulk began. "May I come in, get warmer?" he continued in broken English.

Dixon was excited and nervous.

"Come in," he said and brought his .45 around and put it into his holster as the stranger watched. His hands did not leave the grips of the hand gun. Dixon was unsure of the person's intentions and let the man know by his actions.

The large man lay his rifle against the table. "Thank you," he said. "Okay?" He motioned as if to ask if he could remove his jacket. Dixon nodded his head yes, never taking his eyes off the man.

"Coffee?" Dixon said as he held up a cup.

"Yes, yes," the man said.

Dixon looked at him, wondering where the other person was. He motioned for him to sit down.

Dixon noted the man's enormous size. *Probably six and a half foot tall, three hundred pounds,* he thought. He also noticed a bulge around the waistline that was hid under a brown, insulated sweater. *Probably another gun,* Dixon thought.

"Where did you come from?" Dixon asked.

"Oh, I hunt," he replied. "I am lost. I hike in from lake, but cannot find again."

"The lake is frozen," Dixon said. "How did you get here?"

The man acted like he did not understand Dixon's question.

Dixon looked the man over as he talked. He noticed the outerwear he had on was all new. The man's hands were large but not callused. He had a recent haircut and whiskers were just starting to show on his face.

"What are you hunting for?" Dixon asked, watching the man's eyes.

"Oh, deer or moose," he stammered.

"Where is your partner?" Dixon bluntly asked.

Again, the man shook his head and asked, "What is partner?"

"Your friend, buddy, other man," Dixon replied.

The man's eyes got large and he looked startled by the question. "Oh, I alone, nobody else," he replied.

"Your name?" Dixon repeated. "What's your name?"

The man hesitated. "Name is Emil," he finally said.

Dixon didn't believe anything Emil was telling him. He kept his back to the wall and his hand still on his .45. "How did you get to the lake?" Dixon asked again.

"Guide bring me in boat before water hard," he replied. Dixon just looked at the man; he knew he was lying.

Emil was beginning to show his uneasiness. He stood up and asked, "More coffee please, okay?"

Dixon nodded yes as Emil started toward the stove where the pot had been set.

Dixon walked over to Emil's rifle and picked it up. Emil poured his coffee, and as he turned around to face Dixon, Dixon asked, "Is this a good rifle?"

Emil walked to the table and set his coffee down. He motioned for Dixon to hand him the rifle. "Good rifle," he replied.

Before Dixon handed the rifle to Emil, he ejected three shells. Emil appeared very surprised. "Why you take out?" he asked.

Dixon smiled and replied, "Okay? Okay?"

Emil nodded his head as he sat down.

What do I do now? Dixon pondered as he studied Emil. He didn't trust him, and he sure couldn't let Emil spend the night. "I'll show you the direction to the lake," he told Emil, not believing that is where he came from.

Emil replied, "That good. I go soon." Emil finished his coffee and stood up. "I go now," he said. "Show me lake."

Dixon was relieved but apprehensive. As he reached for the door, he took his hand off his pistol. Emil took two giant strides and with unbelievable speed, grabbed Dixon and threw him to the floor. The impact stunned Dixon, and before he could get up, Emil had taken the .45 out of Dixon's holster. Emil smacked Dixon across the face knocking him out.

A few minutes later, as Dixon was recovering, he realized Emil was tying him up to a support post in the cabin.

"What do you want?" Dixon shouted with blood running out of his nose.

Emil looked down at him. "You good man; just do what we ask, you be okay." Emil opened the door of the cabin, pulled out a whistle and blew three times. In about ten minutes, another person walked through the door. It was a smaller man, his eyes were squinty, dark, and he had permanent frown lines crisscrossing his forehead.

Chapter 29

He and Emil talked to each other in a foreign language. They would look at Dixon as if he were their prize catch. Finally Emil spoke. "You Dixon? Right?"

Dixon did not answer.

They talked to each other again. "We here to get map," Emil said, addressing Dixon. "We know you got map."

Dixon figured as much, so he showed no surprise at their knowledge of his possession. "Maps of what?" Dixon answered. "I live in these woods. I don't need any maps."

"You good man, Dixon," Emil returned, "but we know you have maps. You show us maps and you live. If you don't show us maps, we *make* you tell. Lamier has ways," he continued, as he looked at the other man. "We go tonight. If no maps, you do not live."

"I don't know what maps you're—"

At that, Lamier grabbed Dixon by the jaw and squeezed hard.

"Lamier not want to wait," Emil said. "He will hurt you. Where is maps?"

Dixon just stared at Emil. He knew he had to deal with Emil to survive. Lamier pulled a knife out of his backpack. Lamier said something to Emil, and Emil shook his head no.

"He wants to cut off fingers," Emil said, holding up his four fingers toward Dixon. "You tell me where maps."

Dixon's mind whirled. *They're going to kill me. These guys are from some foreign country with orders to bring the maps back. If I tell them where the maps are, they will kill me anyway.* "They're not here!" Dixon shouted, trying to buy some time.

Emil smiled and spoke to Lamier in their language. Lamier looked at Dixon with hateful and distrustful eyes. "If you do not tell truth," Emil said, "Lamier will be angry. He will cut you."

Dixon appeared to have given into their demands. "It will take two days," Dixon said. "We will have to pack supplies."

Emil again spoke to Lamier. Lamier shook his head violently and shouted "No!" at Dixon. "You lie!" Emil said. "Lamier says you lie!"

"No, no," Dixon shouted back, "you already looked in here two months ago, and you know they're not in here."

Emil looked surprised. "You smart man, Dixon," he said and told Lamier what Dixon had just said. That seemed to pacify Lamier's anger.

Dixon realized they were beginning to believe him.

They talked to each other again, and to Dixon's surprise they started toward the door. Lamier came back and checked Dixon's ropes. They put on their jackets and stepped outside. Dixon couldn't see them from where he was tied. He looked around his cabin. His .45 was lying on the table. Lamier's knife was lying next to it. *I must get loose if I want to live,* he thought. They had done a good job tying his hands, but the rope around his legs and feet was not as tight. He started moving his strong legs in every direction. He could feel the tension of the ropes loosening. He prayed they wouldn't walk back in.

He got his right leg completely loose. He slid down the post so he could throw his leg forward. He wrapped his foot around the table and started to drag it toward him. The friction from the wood table and wood floor rubbing together made a loud screeching sound.

Dixon stopped and held his breath. There were no sounds from outside. *They must have walked away from the cabin,* he thought. He again pulled on the table with his leg. When the table reached his body, he slid his right leg under the tabletop and brought it to his side. He could now reach the tabletop with his right hand. He slid the table to his backside as much as he could. He could feel the knife with his hand. Lamier's knife was sharp.

Dixon maneuvered his hands and cut through the ropes quickly. He freed himself and picked up his gun. It was still loaded! His mind was whirling! There was only one way out of his cabin. *Where were Lamier and Emil?* he wondered. He pulled the door open about two inches. Just as he started searching the area with his eyes, a giant foot slammed open the door. The force almost knocked Dixon over, but he regained his footing. Emil came charging in, yelling apparently at Lamier.

Dixon pulled up his .45 and yelled, "Stop!" to Emil. Emil was getting closer. Dixon could see the anger in his eyes. Dixon pulled the trigger. Emil dropped to his knees with a look of disbelief. He managed to rise up again and stumbled closer to Dixon. Dixon fired again, and Emil was dead. The door was now wide open. Dixon stepped over Emil to peer out. He could not see Lamier. He ran out the door and jumped next to a woodpile. The quiet was eerie.

He had not taken time to put on a jacket. He leaped to the side of his cabin and quickly circled it with the .45 ready to fire. There were no signs of Lamier. He ran back into his cabin and grabbed his outerwear. His courage was building up. He figured Lamier heard the shots and saw Emil on the floor and ran. He had not seen a weapon on Lamier. Dixon went outside again and circled his cabin in a wide pattern.

He continued until he found a single set of footprints going out into the forest. They were Lamier's, he thought, as the footprints were smaller than his own. He went back to his cabin to get his rifle. By now, he felt that Lamier was not a threat.

He decided to get Emil out of the cabin. He pulled up Emil's bulging sweater and pulled out a 9mm pistol. Emil's rifle was still standing against the wall. He put the 9mm on his waist and emptied the shells out of Emil's rifle again.

Dragging Emil was like dragging a large moose. Dixon had poles with rudders made for that purpose. He rolled Emil onto the primitive gurney and slid him out of the cabin door with ease. He pulled him away from the cabin until he was exhausted.

Emil will freeze now, Dixon thought. *I'll take care of his body later.*

It was beginning to snow again. Dixon didn't know whether Lamier knew that he would be tracking him, but surely he'd notice that the new snow would cover his prints.

Chapter 30

After he saw Emil go down, Lamier fled fast. He had neglected to pick up his snowshoes, though, and the traveling was slow. He remembered Emil had told Dixon that they would go that night. *Does the American know how we came in?* he wondered. *Or maybe he even knows where we landed . . . I must complete my assignment! If I go back without the maps, I must make sure the widower is dead. These were the orders!*

* * *

Dixon followed the footprints until he could no longer see them. He headed back to the cabin. He didn't think Lamier was armed, but he wasn't taking any chances. *Lamier was a cunning, smart little weasel,* Dixon thought. *If the copter is coming back tonight, Lamier might be back to try to kill me.* He could tell when he returned to the cabin that Lamier had not returned before he did. He wondered if Emil and Lamier had set up a camp nearby when they arrived, and if they had food . . . and maybe more weapons that Lamier could pick up.

Dixon didn't want to be caught in the cabin without an escape plan. He went to the outside rear of his cabin. He removed the pine branches he had stacked and cut an opening large enough to crawl through. He recovered the opening with pine branches and went inside and put his bearskin rug over the hole. He pulled some beef jerky from his shelves and put his coffeepot on the stove.

If Lamier doesn't come back here, I'm going back to where that copter landed before, he thought. *I don't know what I'll do, but I have to know when—or if—Lamier gets back on it.*

Drinking his coffee and watching the fire, his thoughts turned to Chris again. First it was her death, and then he found Luke murdered. Back in Dovel, a nasty divorce and old friends had changed and acted mysteriously. Then, the information from Jerry about Frank Norris and his strange antics. Now another man was dead in his backyard, and another one was probably lurking nearby.

And it all goes back to the maps! Then I told Jerry and Cody about the maps. Their lives could be in danger. He walked back outside. There were no signs of footprints. When he walked back into his cabin, he decided to do something that he couldn't believe, himself, of ever doing. *I am going to burn the maps!* he thought. *I will write down they have been destroyed in case I do not survive. Maybe lives will be saved if it is known the maps no longer exist.* He pulled the maps from their hiding place. He looked at them with tears streaming down his face. "Chris, Chris!" he called as he threw the maps into the fiery stove.

He put on his outer gear, picked up his rifle, and started toward the spot where the copter landed two days ago. He had only begun his hike when he heard the familiar copter blades whirling. *They're landing close to my cabin!* he thought.

He turned around and watched the military type copter lower itself to the ground within a hundred yards of his cabin. He moved to get a better view, looking for Lamier to step out from nowhere. No one deplaned from the copter until the blades completely stopped. It looked like the copter had several passengers. There were voices shouting as they got out of the copter.

"Dixon! Dixon!" they were shouting. It wasn't until they got closer that Dixon recognized Cody.

"Cody!" he yelled, and they ran to each other and embraced.

"What are you doing here?" Dixon exclaimed. Cody motioned to two men who were approaching. "This is Dwight Cox, special agent for the FBI, and this is Wendall Hartzel, from the CIA. We got a lot of talking to do, and these guys are on our side. Before you and I talk, they want to ask you some questions."

"Dixon," Hartzel said, "have you seen another copter in this area in the last two days?"

"Yes!" Dixon replied looking puzzled at Hartzel.

"Have you encountered anyone?" he continued.

"I sure have," Dixon replied, starting to walk. "Let me show you something."

He led them to Emil's body and brushed away the snow.

Hartzel stepped back and looked at Cox. "Emil," he said, "anyone else?"

"There's another guy out here called Lamier," Dixon said. "The other copter is planning to pick him up tonight!"

"Do you know where?" Hartzel asked.

"I think so," Dixon replied. "I was just headed that way. If we start now, we should be there in time. I figured they'll land close to sundown."

"Where is Lamier?" Cox asked.

"Well, he was probably close by until you landed," Dixon replied. "We were playing cat-and-mouse."

"Hey," Hartzel exclaimed. "Emil and Lamier have been partners for years. They are professional killers . . . or were," he chuckled.

He told the copter pilot to hide the copter. "I don't want to scare them away," he exclaimed. "Let's get started!"

They had walked for half an hour when Dixon spotted an unusual color ahead. He motioned for the rest to lay low. He pointed toward a large red spot on the snow up ahead. He pulled his .45 and Hartzel pulled his 7mm. They approached the area from both sides.

When they saw what it was, Hartzel and Dixon shivered. They shouted for the others to come ahead. They had found Lamier! He had been torn open by coyotes. Their tracks were everywhere. They covered his body with pine boughs. If a copter was coming in, it would have spotted the red and not landed.

They approached the area where Dixon had found the copter runner prints and waited. Just before sundown, the sound of whirling blades was heard; then there appeared a large black copter. It was a military type copter as well, armed with machine guns.

Hartzel had planned well. The CIA had known a helicopter had been in the Ticonderoga area. That was one of the reasons they had flown into Dixon's camp.

He brought with him a three-quarter-inch cable with hooks on each end. When the copter landed, he crawled under it from the back where he couldn't be seen. He looped the cable around the two axles of the copter and looped the other end around a large tree. The two men in the copter finally turned off the engine. They were waiting for Emil and Lamier.

Hartzel yelled to the two men, "Sorino! Sorino!" which meant surrender in their language.

The engine immediately began to turn the large blades. In a few seconds, they attempted to lift off, but the cable held. They jumped out of the copter with small machine guns blazing in all directions. Hartzel and Cox returned fire and had to kill both men.

Having accounted for every one of the intruders, they returned to the cabin, where Hartzel and Cox explained to Dixon their role throughout this investigation. They explained briefly what had happened in Dovel with Ted and Tara—how they reached Cody and convinced him of the possible danger you were in.

Dixon paused. "I just burned the maps up," he said, pulling out fragments of charred paper from his stove. "I guess I'm glad I did."

Hartzel and Cox looked at each other and shrugged their shoulders. "We will close this case as of today, Dixon," Hartzel said. "I'm glad you burned up those cursed maps." We will put a classified memo out that we know will be intercepted by the radicals who are behind all of this. The memo will include our visit to the Ticonderoga and our discussion with you about the destruction of the maps. We will officially close this case, and that will convince the radicals that it is over."

Cody spoke up. "Dixon, do you want a ride back to Shaloh? Linda will be cooking up a storm."

"Sure," Dixon replied. "I am finished with the Ticonderoga! I'll never return."

The first call Dixon made when he returned to Shaloh was to Mary Jo. "I'm coming home to stay," he said.

She screamed with joy.